Stage Fright

For Chloe & Holly B

STRIPES PUBLISHING
An imprint of Little Tiger Press
1 The Coda Centre, 189 Munster Road,
London SW6 6AW

A paperback original
First published in Great Britain in 2012

Text copyright © Belinda Rapley, 2012
Cover illustration © Joe Berger, 2012

ISBN: 978-1-84715-239-8

The right of Belinda Rapley to be identified
as the author of this work has been asserted by
her in accordance with the Copyright,
Designs and Patents Act, 1988.

A CIP catalogue record for this book is
available from the British Library.

Printed and bound in the UK.

10 9 8 7 6 5 4 3 2 1

Holly Robbins

BFFs

Stage Fright

Stripes

Ghoulish goings-on at Lexie's Halloween Party

"You two look a bit green – are you sure you're feeling OK?" Dad joked as we drove through town on our way to Lexie's Halloween sleepover. He glanced in the rear-view mirror at Jas, and shook his head with a wry smile.

Jas adjusted her pointy black hat and gave him her best witchy grin. "Watch out, Mr Lovewood, or I might turn you into a frog!"

"Yeah, an ugly, green, warty one!" I giggled.

Jas and I were the mirror image of each other. We'd gone into town the day before to buy Halloween make-up kits and now we were dressed as identical

witches – stripy green-and-black tights, black dresses with floaty sleeves, green faces and pointy hats.

"Brownlow Road. We're here!" Jas said excitedly, peering out of the window as Dad turned the corner.

I nodded, but inside I felt a tiny bit nervous. Jas had made friends with Lexie and Nisha during the first half term at our new secondary school, Priory Road, after me and Jas had fallen out big time. The three of them had hung out loads while we weren't talking, so she knew them much better than I did. The last sleepover I'd been to was at Kirsty's – the most über-cool girl in our class – and the whole thing had been a total nightmare from start to finish.

"Look, number fifty-seven – that's Lexie's house!" said Jas.

Dad pulled up in front of a slightly ramshackle terraced house. As soon as he switched off the engine, Jas flung open her door and leaped out, grabbing her overnight bag. She pulled open the garden gate and raced up the path, almost tripping over in her mum's black pointy shoes that she'd stuffed full of newspaper to make them fit. I hung back, clutching my bag, suddenly feeling a bit of an outsider.

Jas rang the doorbell, then turned round to chivvy

me along – and noticed the look on my face.

"Come on, Ellie," said Jas, doubling back and linking her arm through mine. "You'll be fine," she encouraged, reading my mind as usual. "You know what great fun Lexie and Nisha are."

"I know," I replied, trying to calm my nerves. "I'm looking forward to getting to know them a bit better."

Suddenly we heard lots of barking from inside the house. The next second, the front door was pulled open and two huge chocolate Labradors barged past Lexie and bounded towards us, wagging their tails and leaping up to say hello. I giggled as their raspy tongues tickled my hands.

"Eeeurgh!" Jas squealed.

"Smarty! Jinx! Down!" Lexie called out, grabbing their collars and leading them back into the house. "Hi, guys! Come on in. Happy Halloween!"

"You, too!" said Jas. "*Wizard* outfit!"

Lexie was wearing a long black cape decorated with shiny silver stars and moons, and a matching pointy hat. A long flowing white wig covered her usually scruffy pony tail and she was holding a wand.

I smiled. "You look a bit like Wiggy!"

We giggled, thinking of our geography teacher,

Mr Wigglesworth, with his slightly crazy grey hair.

We followed Lexie into the hallway. Two muddy bikes leaned against the wall on one side, whilst on the other a vast collection of shoes and trainers were piled up below an overflowing coat rack. Nisha appeared from the kitchen, her long glossy black hair pulled back into a sleek pony tail.

"Wow! Your outfit is amazing!" Jas beamed, admiring Nisha's all-in-one black jumpsuit, which had the bones of a skeleton painted in white on it.

"The bones glow in the dark, too," Nisha explained shyly. "I painted them on myself!"

"Cool!" I said, seriously impressed. As we patted and stroked the dogs, a tall woman dressed in jeans and a hoody appeared in the hallway. She had the same bright blue eyes and messy hair as Lexie.

"Lexie, the dogs are supposed to stay in the kitchen." She shooed them inside and shut the door. "Sorry about that. You must be Jas and Ellie," she said, smiling. Jas beamed and I nodded. "And you must be Ellie's dad."

"Guilty," Dad laughed.

Lexie grabbed my arm. "Come on, let's leave the oldies to it. You've got to come and see my treehouse!"

Stage Fright

"Hang on," Mrs Jones said firmly. "Bags upstairs first, please. This house is enough of a muddle already without *more* clutter in the hallway!"

Lexie groaned, then led the way upstairs. Her room was at the end of a wide, uncarpeted landing, with bare walls except for tiny patches of colour dotted here and there.

"Dad's been decorating this house since we moved in three years ago," Lexie explained, as she shoved her door open to reveal a large, square room with bold blue walls. The wardrobe in the corner was crammed with clothes that were spilling out of it. There was a big bed along one wall, with magazines and boot-slippers poking out from underneath; beside it was a haphazard row of blow-up beds topped with duvets and pillows.

"It's not normally this neat," Lexie said, looking round disapprovingly. "Mum made me tidy up in your honour."

"Home from home!" Jas beamed, dumping her bag on the floor and joining Nisha and Lexie at the window to check out the treehouse.

"Wow!" said Jas. "Come and see, Ellie!"

I put down my bag and hurried over. It was dark

outside, but on one side of the garden, framed with fairy lights, was a huge round-turreted treehouse. It wasn't actually in a tree, but on stilts raising it about two metres from the ground. I could just make out a ladder at the front. At the back of the garden, flames from a bonfire licked the night sky.

"It's magical!" I breathed. "I think I'd like to live there."

"Unfortunately I have to share it with Luke," Lexie said. "Otherwise I might!"

At that moment we heard the dogs barking excitedly. "That'll be Dad and Luke now – they've been at football practice," Lexie said. "To the treehouse, quick!"

We flew back along the landing, and piled down the stairs. Dad was shaking Lexie's dad's hand and chatting about football as Luke yanked off his muddy boots and flung them by the door. Luke was Lexie's twin brother – I recognized him from school, although he was in Goldfinch, not Kingfisher with us. He was a LOT more shy than Lexie.

"I'm off now, Ellie," Dad called out. "See you tomorrow – and remember to get some sleep!"

"OK, OK," I said, giving him a quick hug. "Bye!"

Jas was waiting for me by the back door. As we

Stage Fright

followed the others out into the darkening night, Jas did a mad witch's dance ("I'm casting a spell!"). Lexie shinned up the ladder first and the rest of us bundled after her, with me and Jas tripping over our flowing black dresses. There were more fairy lights inside and a couple of bright lamps. Big, squishy floor cushions lined the walls and a glass bowl of mysterious green liquid sat on a round table alongside four glasses.

"I made this myself," said Lexie, using a ladle to fill the glasses. "Looks good, doesn't it?"

"No, Lexie, it looks revolting," said Jas, making a face as she sniffed hers suspiciously. "What is it?!"

"Beetle-juice," Lexie said ghoulishly, just as we all took a sip. I nearly spluttered mine everywhere.

"Careful!" Jas giggled as I managed to get myself back under control and swallow. "You don't want a repeat performance of what happened in the diner!"

"Uh, don't remind me," I grimaced, my heart racing for a second as I thought back to one of the many disasters in my first half term at Priory Road.

"I still can't believe you sprayed root beer all over the coolest guy in school!" Nisha giggled.

"Shame you didn't get Kirsty, too," Lexie grinned, taking a gulp of her green drink.

I bit my lip, then started to smile. At least they all thought it was funny rather than tragic. "Last half term really couldn't have got much worse," I cringed, ticking the incidents off on my fingers. "There was my new nickname from Ed – Woodworm ... two detentions from the fiercest teacher in the school..."

"And the time you got caught wearing make-up," Jas added helpfully.

"Not to mention you two falling out big time," Lexie said, looking a bit more serious.

"This half term we should make a pact," Nisha suggested, "that we won't fall out."

"No matter what," I agreed, looking at Jas. Luckily we'd got our friendship back on track, but it had been the most miserable two weeks of my life and I never wanted that to happen again. "This half term *has* to be better, anyway."

Jas smiled knowingly. "I've got a feeling that it's going to be awesome! There's tons to look forward to."

Nisha frowned. "Like what?"

"There's my birthday for a start!" Jas beamed. "The sixteenth of December, in case you'd forgotten! And it's Christmas, so there's bound to be lots of festive stuff going on, and Josh says there's an end-of-term disco. And best of all, there's the school play – *Oliver!*."

"Are you going to audition?" Nisha asked.

Jas nodded. "Defo. I really want a starring role, but Josh reckons that no one in Year Seven or Eight ever gets cast as a lead."

"I guess he'd know, wouldn't he?" I said. Jas's older brother was in Year Nine, and loved the fact that he knew more than we did about life at Priory Road.

Jas looked concerned for about a millisecond, then shrugged. "I'll just have to do the most show-stoppingly amazing audition – then Mrs Crawfield won't have any choice but to give me a star part!"

"Are you two auditioning?" I asked, looking anxiously at Nisha and Lexie. They glanced at each other, then nodded, grinning.

"Only for the chorus, though," Lexie said.

"How about you?"

I shook my head. I hated being in the spotlight. "The most acting I've ever done is playing the third sheep in a nativity play at Woodview," I said. "There's no way I'd do anything at Priory – it would be terrifying!"

"Are you sure?" Jas asked. "It would be so much fun if we could all go to rehearsals together."

I shook my head. "Sorry! Not even for you, Jas!"

"Maybe you could still be involved somehow," Nisha suggested, "even if it's not on the stage."

"Yeah, they're bound to need backstage crew," said Lexie.

At that moment we heard footsteps outside in the dark, making me and Nisha jump.

"Ghosts!" Lexie whispered dramatically.

"It's me, idiot," we heard Luke mutter from the bottom of the ladder. "Mum told me to tell you that the jacket potatoes are ready."

Lexie sighed dramatically. "Brothers! They are total pains."

"Too right," Jas giggled. "You are so lucky you don't have one, Ellie."

We followed Lexie down the ladder and back across the garden to the kitchen. The baked potatoes smelled delicious – they'd been finished off in the bonfire and were wrapped in silver foil. We piled them with cheese and beans, then carried them back up into the treehouse, chatting between mouthfuls about what else we'd got up to during the holiday.

After we'd eaten, Lexie switched off the lights and we all fell silent. It was pitch-black, except for the glow of Nisha's skeleton costume.

"Er, Lexie," Nisha whispered. "What are you doing?"

Lexie rustled around in the dark for a second, before suddenly switching on a big torch. She held it under her chin, pointing the beam upwards so that it lit up her face, in a strange, shadowy way.

"Time for ghost stories!" she said in a spooky voice, making us all giggle. We took it in turns to tell a scary story, but when it came round to me my head went blank. "I can't remember any," I squeaked.

"Make one up, Ellie," Jas suggested. "You've got the best imagination ever and you're brilliant at writing stories."

"OK then," I said, "I'll give it a go..."

Lexie and Nisha nestled further down into their big cushions, waiting for me to begin.

I took a deep breath. "It was a cold, dark night, and four friends were messing about in a treehouse at the end of the garden when they heard a thin, piercing howl..."

I got really into it, making the story as scary as I could. Just as I reached the terrifying climax an owl hooted outside. Everyone jumped, including me,

then we dissolved into silent hysterics. We'd nearly recovered when a twig snapped outside. We all squealed and grabbed hold of each other, totally spooked.

"What's going on up there?" The familiar voice of Lexie's mum sent us into a fresh wave of relieved giggles. Her face appeared at the top of the ladder. "Come on, time for bed."

"Already?" Lexie groaned.

"Yes, and no arguments, please," said Mrs Jones firmly. We piled up our plates and carried them down the ladder. As we walked across the garden, the moon cast spooky shadows on the lawn, making me shiver.

"This is like your story, Ellie!" Nisha whispered, glancing over her shoulder anxiously. "Four girls being stalked by a restless ghoul!"

"Time to walk a bit faster," I said, forgetting for a second that I'd made the whole thing up. By the time we reached the back door we were all running. We tumbled into the warm kitchen, breathless and giggling. Jinx and Smarty were lounging in their baskets – they looked up and thumped their tails against the floor in greeting.

"Luke's already in bed," Lexie's dad said. "So try not

to be too loud."

"Dad, it's a sleepover," Lexie said. "You can't expect us to be quiet!"

"Just keep it down, OK? And make sure you shut your door."

"We will, Mr Jones," Nisha said politely as we followed Lexie upstairs.

Jas and I went to the bathroom to clean off our green make-up.

"Not feeling nervous any more?" said Jas as she scrubbed at her face.

I smiled and shook my head. "I'm having the best time *ever*, even if I have turned my face permanently green. This make-up is seriously hard to get off!"

After washing our faces four times, we hurried back along the landing to Lexie's room. We got changed into our pyjamas and snuggled down under the duvets. I was between Nisha and Jas and I noticed Nisha pull a soft, floppy rabbit from her bag. She caught me looking.

Nisha blushed. "Meet Flopsy. She always sleeps with me."

"She's really sweet!" I said. "I normally sleep with a huge tabby cat, but I couldn't fit him in my bag!"

Lexie giggled. "That's just as well, really – I'm not sure how friendly Jinx and Smarty would have been."

We talked and talked, until there were longer gaps between our whispers. Finally I started to yawn and I could hear Nisha yawning, too. Then Jas started to snore lightly and suddenly the room fell silent. As I lay there in the dark I smiled to myself; I couldn't believe I'd been nervous about the sleepover, it was so much more relaxed and fun than Kirsty's. Lexie and Nisha were so friendly. Lexie was a bit like Jas, loud and outgoing, whereas Nisha was more quiet and thoughtful, a bit more like me. But I reckoned Jas was right – this half term was going to be fab, with the four of us hanging out together as BFFs!

The next morning, I was woken by the sound of Jas squealing next to me. I turned over and squinted up at her.

"What's up?" I asked croakily, as Nisha stirred on my other side.

"I've forgotten my normal clothes!" Jas groaned, frantically rummaging through her bag.

Me and Nisha began to giggle and Lexie nearly fell

out of her bed from laughing so much.

Jas's face broke into a grin. "Oh well, I guess I'm going home in my pyjamas and a witch's hat then."

"Good job we're getting a lift!" I spluttered.

Mum arrived to pick us up, just as we were finishing breakfast. We fetched our stuff and thanked Mrs Jones for having us.

"See you on Monday!" Jas cried, as we said our goodbyes in the hall.

"Ugh, I've got a ton of homework to do before then," Lexie grumbled.

"Should have done it last weekend like I did," said Luke, appearing in the hallway and grabbing his football boots. He smiled smugly, going a bit pink at the same time, and headed out of the door.

"Goody two-shoes," Lexie muttered.

"I've almost done it all," Nisha said, sounding relieved. "I've just got English to finish."

"Me, too," I said.

"I've been too busy watching the *Oliver!* DVD, ready for the auditions," Jas explained. "I forgot all about homework! I guess that's my Sunday gone!"

And with a final goodbye we headed for the car, Jas shuffling along in her PJs and pointy shoes.

I get another party invite, but there's bad news about the end-of-term disco

After a half-term holiday filled with lie-ins, it was a real struggle to get up when my alarm went off on Monday morning. I was about to snooze it and pull the duvet over my head when Dad appeared.

"Wake up, sleepyhead!" He came over to the bed and ruffled Crumble's fur. "That goes for you, too, lazybones." He clunked a glass of orange juice down on my bedside table, then pulled back my curtains, revealing a wet and miserable morning.

"So, are you raring to get to school?" he asked.

"I wouldn't go that far," I said sleepily, rubbing my eyes. Then I thought about it for a second. "But I am looking forward to seeing everyone again."

"That's my Shrimp," he smiled. I groaned at the nickname, even though it fitted me pretty well – not just because I was small, but because I was shy and had a habit of blushing pink all the time. He disappeared out of the door, whistling as he went.

"Lucky Crumble, you can laze around all day," I yawned as I slid out of bed. Ten minutes later, I was dressed and staring at myself in the mirror.

"I'm still tiny and my uniform's still huge and baggy," I moaned to Crumble. "When am I going to start growing?!"

At least I knew I wasn't the only one rocking the "oversized uniform" look – there were at least five others in Kingfisher alone who had the same problem. I hurried downstairs and into the kitchen.

"Oooh, pancakes!" I said. "My favourite – thanks, Mum!"

Mum smiled as she put blueberries and yoghurt on the table. "I thought I'd treat you, as it's your first day back."

"I'm actually kind of looking forward to it, in a weird way," I said as I tucked in.

Mum looked sideways at me. "Really?" I nodded

and she smiled warmly. "That's brilliant, Ellie." I guess she was a bit worried after all of the problems I had in the first half term, but things were different now. Jas and I were friends again and we had Lexie and Nisha to hang out with, too.

Breakfast over, I disappeared into the hall and shoved my books in my bag. At least I'd be heading into school today with the cool purple one, rather than the monstrous black one Mum had insisted on when I started at Priory Road.

Dad rushed in and grabbed his keys. "See you all later," he said, hurrying out of the door. "Have a great day, Shrimp."

"I better get going, too," I said, tugging on my coat and stepping out into the damp, drizzly morning. Mum waved me off from the door, then I pulled up my hood and raced round the corner to Jas's flat. She was standing at the door waiting for me.

"Did you manage to get your homework done?" I asked, as she ran out to meet me. Jas shook her head, looking sheepish.

"I just couldn't concentrate on anything else apart from *Oliver!*," she said. "I'm going to have to do some on the bus or I'll be in big trouble."

Stage Fright

"I can help," I offered.

"Thanks," she said gratefully, as we reached the bus stop. Josh was already there with his mates. He was still insisting on his "no talking to Year Sevens" rule, but he did look in our direction and give me a nod just as the bus appeared. We scrambled to the back and grabbed a seat each. Jas dragged out her maths books and puzzled over the equations we'd been set before half term. I helped where I could, but we were both as confused as each other when it came to maths. Next she scribbled down a few sentences for her history homework, her handwriting wobbling as the bus jerked forward or went over a pothole, but she was so distracted, humming the *Oliver!* tunes, that she didn't finish it before we arrived. She shoved her books away and we hurried off the bus, joining the throng of Priory Road children on the pavement. I heard heavy footsteps behind me and turned to see Ed appear at our shoulders. Zac lumbered along behind.

"Welcome back, Woody!" Ed grinned, slowing down as he reached us. "Good holiday?"

"Better than being at school," I said.

"Bet you both missed me, though," he said, as Zac guffawed.

"Yeah, right, Ed," Jas said, shaking her head, but she couldn't help smiling.

"I knew it!" he said. "Should've come to the skate park – I was there all week learning some serious moves."

"Did you manage to stay on this time?" I joked, remembering the last time we'd seen Ed and Zac on their boards; they'd been showing off, trying to look cool, when Ed had flipped his over and landed on his back!

"Ha ha, very funny!" Ed grinned. "See you in registration, Woody."

They sped ahead of us and fell into step with Ajay, Travis and Dev. Jas smiled. "Woody's an improvement on Woodworm, at least."

"I suppose it is," I agreed as we reached the huge iron gates that had scared me so much back in September.

"Oh, no," I said, suddenly faltering. "There's Kirsty and Eliza."

"Looking as frosty as ever," Jas added. Jas hadn't trusted Kirsty from the day she'd first set eyes on her, and her judgement had turned out to be right. Before half term Kirsty had acted like my best friend, but it turned out she only wanted to be friends so I'd help her get good marks in English. And it had taken Jas to point this out to me. Jas linked my arm protectively, just as Kirsty looked over, wrinkling her button nose in disdain.

"Just ignore her," Jas said, loudly enough for her to hear. I saw Kirsty huff.

"I don't know why I thought she was so cool," I said quietly, as we hurried past.

"Exactly, she's a Year Seven, same as us," Jas pointed out as we spotted Lexie and Nisha waving through the crowd. We hurried over and walked through the main doors together.

"It feels so good to walk in here knowing where we're going," Lexie said, as we dumped our coats in the noisy cloakroom and headed back into the corridor. Then for a second she looked up, confused. "Err, which way is 1F again?"

We all burst into giggles.

"Well, the lockers are definitely in this direction," said Nisha, pulling us down the corridor.

"Before we get there, I've got something for you guys," Jas said, delving into her bag. She pulled out a bundle of little purple envelopes and handed them out.

"Ooooh, exciting!" Nisha said, as we quickly opened them.

*You are invited to a day of Dancing on Ice
to celebrate Jasmine Cole's 12th birthday!
3rd December, 11am–3pm, including lunch.
Hope you can make it!*
RSVP

"Wow, Jas! A skating party – how cool is that?" I said, giving her a hug.

"I'm going to invite a few of the other girls from our class," Jas said excitedly, "but I wanted to give you yours first because I was hoping you could come back after the ice skating for a sleepover. Mum said three's the limit. Can you come?"

"Absolutely," said Lexie.

"Count me in!" said Nisha.

"Of course!" I grinned.

As we checked out the invites, Jas saw Trin, Tabitha and Molly up ahead, and rushed over.

"Yay! Ice skating!" Molly beamed as she read the invite. "That's such a great idea, Jas!"

"I've never been before," Trin said anxiously, "is it really hard?"

"Only when you fall on the ice," Lexie giggled.

Stage Fright

With Nisha leading, we found our way to 1F. Kirsty glided in behind us, her nose in the air, and sat down next to Zophia.

"That's awkward," Jas whispered to me as we took our seats. "I've got an invite for Zophia, but not for Kirsty."

"Funnily enough," Lexie whispered over her shoulder, as she and Nisha sat down in front of us. The next moment, Miss Dubois, our form tutor, arrived. She was wearing a pinstripe suit and high heels, and her wavy brown hair was swept back off her face in a high pony tail. She smiled warmly and waited for everyone to stop talking.

"*Bonjour* 1F," she began in her soft French accent. "I hope you enjoyed your holiday and are all glad to be back, *oui*?"

The class groaned, although when I looked round everyone was smiling except for Kirsty. But then she never did.

"Now," Miss Dubois continued, "I know you're all keen to get to double PE, but first, I've got some exciting announcements to make."

"She's talking about *Oliver!* – I know she is!" Jas whispered, nudging me with her elbow. "She might

know about the auditions!"

"First of all, as I'm sure you already know, the school play this term will be *Oliver!*. Auditions will be taking place very soon, so keep an eye on the noticeboard to find out all the details. I hope lots of you will get involved. And if acting isn't for you, Mrs Crawfield will need lots of volunteers to help with costumes, make-up and other backstage jobs, so there's something for everyone."

"That's perfect, Ellie," Nisha said, turning round to face me. "If you help out backstage you can still come to the rehearsals!"

I smiled at the possibility as the rest of the class began chattering excitedly. Miss Dubois waited for everyone to quieten down.

"Next, I have a competition to tell you about," she said. "Every year, we ask all the students to design a Christmas card and the winning entry from each year is printed and sold to raise money for the school. Mr Thompson, head of art, will be the judge and there will be an opportunity to use the art rooms during lunchtimes to work on your designs. I know we have some talented artists in this form, so I hope you will all have a go."

Stage Fright

In front of us, Lexie nudged Nisha, and I heard her say, "You have *so* got to enter that, Nish!"

As the excited chatter started up again, there was a loud cough, and Kirsty piped up. "Miss Dubois, we *are* having a school disco this term, aren't we? It's not going to *all* be babyish competitions and stuff, is it?"

Miss Dubois took a deep breath and smiled at Kirsty, as if she wanted to say something, but had thought better of it.

"That's because she's got a new Year Nine crush," Zac guffawed, making smoochy-smoochy faces, "and she wants a slow dance!"

"Ah, Crusty!" Ed called out, using his new nickname for her. "I thought it was me you liked!"

"Ugh, in your dreams," Kirsty replied sniffily.

"Nightmares, more like," Zac joked, making the class giggle.

"If everyone can settle down," Miss Dubois said, "I was just getting round to that, thank you, Kirsty. Last year we thought that the disco was a little too *grande*," she said, "and it went on quite late. So this year we've decided to have two discos – a junior one for Year Seven and Eight, and a senior one for Year Nine and above."

"What?" cried Kirsty. "That's so unfair!"

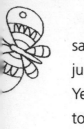

"That's enough, thank you, Kirsty," Miss Dubois said, giving her a stern look. "I will be organizing the junior disco, along with the other form teachers from Year Seven and Eight and we thought it would be fun to have a theme. So, I'm going to put a suggestions box on my desk and you can drop in any ideas you have." She looked at her watch. "Right, you'd better all get going, or you'll be late for PE."

At breaktime we bumped into Josh in the corridor heading to the lockers. As soon as he saw us, his face cracked into the most humungous grin.

"I hear the babies are having their own little disco this year," he smirked. "Sweet!"

"Ugh, don't, Josh," Jas muttered. "We're seriously unimpressed."

"We've got to come up with a theme, too," Lexie added. She didn't seem at all shy of Josh, although I noticed that Nisha looked a bit awkward. "What's wrong with just music and dancing?"

"We're getting a DJ," Josh bragged. "Oh, and it goes on a whole hour longer than yours. Reckon you'll get jelly and ice cream?" Josh winked at us, then turned and sauntered off down the corridor in search of his mates.

We headed for the playground to look for Maisie and Zophia, so that Jas could hand out the last of her birthday invites. Then we bundled into the cloakroom to help her with her history homework before racing to the next lesson.

"I know we've only been away for a week," I puffed as we pushed open the classroom door, "but I'd forgotten how hectic Priory Road is!"

"Me too," Nisha groaned as she slumped into her chair.

The rest of the day was a blur of lessons. When the final bell went we grabbed our coats and rushed outside into the cold afternoon. We said goodbye to Nisha and Lexie and made our way to the bus stop.

"I hope the posters go up about the auditions tomorrow," Jas said excitedly, linking arms with me. "I can't wait to start rehearsals, it'll be so much fun!"

"Maybe Mrs Crawfield will tell us about it during drama club tomorrow," I said, feeling a flutter of nerves as the bus pulled up and we jumped on.

"I still can't believe your dad let you give up your Wednesday swimming session so you could join

drama," Jas said as we found ourselves a seat downstairs. "It'll be so great to have you there."

"Thanks, Jas," I said, nervously twiddling the strap on my bag.

I looked out of the window and noticed Jas looking at me with a puzzled look on her face. "What's up, Ellie?"

"I'm just being silly," I admitted, "but I'm still terrified of getting up on stage and performing in front of anyone, let alone the whole drama club and Mrs Crawfield..."

"Mrs Crawfield won't make you do anything you don't want to," Jas smiled, reassuringly. "Anyway – you might suddenly find your calling and transform into a real diva after a few classes, who knows?!"

"Nooo, then I'll be just like you," I groaned, laughing.

I join drama club and get asked a tricky question by my BFF

Tuesday dragged by, but finally we made it to the last lesson of the day: art. Miss Malik let us make a start on our Christmas card designs and Nisha spent ages sketching out some rough ideas.

"You're taking this very seriously," Jas said, peeping over her shoulder.

"No more so than you are with the play," Nisha pointed out.

"Ooh, touché!" Lexie laughed. "You're just both really lucky that there's something you feel so passionate about. And you've got swimming, Ellie. What have I got?"

"Er, cross country!" Jas joked.

Mrs Townsend, or Terrifying Townsend as Jas had nicknamed her, had singled Lexie out as a potential medal winner and had insisted on her joining the cross-country team, much to Lexie's horror.

"Ha ha, very funny," said Lexie, but she was smiling in spite of herself.

The bell went and we quickly packed up and headed to the hall. Mrs Crawfield was already there, surrounded by a big group of kids.

After a couple of minutes, she climbed the stairs to the stage, and waited for everyone to fall silent.

"How lovely to see so many familiar faces," she said in her clear, sing-song voice, "and I notice there are a few new members amongst the throng, too."

I felt my heart skip as Jas turned to me and smiled.

"Now, I've already had lots of questions about *Oliver!*," Mrs Crawfield continued. "I'm very impressed by how much interest there is in our Christmas play – Priory Road productions are renowned for their flair and professionalism, and I'm sure this year will be no exception."

An excited buzz filled the hall and Jas gripped my arm tightly. "Ow!" I yelped.

"Sorry," she whispered, "I'm just so excited!"

"A poster will go up in the foyer tomorrow with details of the auditions, which will be held next Monday," Mrs Crawfield explained, glancing round the room. "I hope you'll all have a go, because we'll be using this Tuesday evening slot as rehearsal time from the week after next. Now, on to what we're doing this evening. Let's start with our usual warm-up…"

"Did you see that?" Jas whispered urgently.

"What?" I whispered back as Lexie and Nisha leaned in so they could hear, too.

"That look Mrs Crawfield just gave me when she was talking about the auditions," Jas said, her eyes almost popping out of her head as everyone else began to get into pairs. "I'm sure it was a sign!"

"A sign of what?" Nisha asked, frowning. All around us, pairs of children began to pretend they were looking in a mirror, with one mimicking the other.

"That she wants me to audition, of course," Jas said. She gasped suddenly, her eyes widening. "I wonder if she's earmarked me for one of the lead roles?!"

"I doubt it, Jas. Mrs Crawfield was goggling everyone," Lexie pointed out bluntly. "She even looked at me, and I'm pretty sure I'm not a shoo-in

for Nancy or Oliver!"

My mouth dropped open as I saw Jas bristle. She wasn't used to being contradicted; I never pulled her up when she was being over the top – after all, it was just Jas being Jas.

"Come on," Nisha said, looking as uncomfortable as me, "we'd better get started. Lexie, do you want to partner up?"

"Girls, time to warm up, not chat!" Mrs Crawfield called out from the stage, looking over disapprovingly. I went pink and grabbed Jas quickly. Thankfully it didn't take long for her to forget Lexie's words, and within a few minutes she was pulling increasingly mad poses for me to copy. Soon everyone around us was in giggles.

"Jasmine, or should I say 'Joker Jasmine' – clowning is a good dramatic skill to have but there's a time and a place for everything. This is a serious exercise," Mrs Crawfield said sternly. "Concentrate, please."

After we'd warmed up, Mrs Crawfield pulled out a copy of the *Oliver!* script and asked us to think about the motivation for each of the main characters. Jas settled down immediately and stayed focused until the class ended. As we rushed out into the darkening evening, she was bubbling over with excitement.

"This play's going to be incredible," she babbled. "Now Mrs Crawfield's given us some help, I'm going to practise getting into character so I'm ready for Monday."

"How did you get on, Ellie?" Nisha asked. "Did you enjoy your first drama club?"

I nodded. "Yeah, it was great, thanks, but there's still no way I'm auditioning for the play! I'd rather eat Wiggy's hairpiece than get up on that stage." As Jas, Lexie and Nisha shrieked with laughter, Dad's car came into view.

"So, how are the budding actors?" he asked as we all piled inside. We giggled and he smiled when he saw my glowing, happy face. I guess if he needed confirmation that letting me off swimming was a good idea, he'd just got it.

After Dad dropped Lexie and Nisha off, Jas leaned forward in her seat. She was looking more thoughtful than usual.

"What's up?" I asked.

"Do you think Lexie was right earlier?" she asked. "About Mrs Crawfield looking at everyone, I mean?"

"Erm, maybe," I said, squirming a bit as Jas's shoulders drooped. I knew how much getting a lead

role meant to her and I couldn't bear to be the one to burst her bubble. "But who knows," I gabbled. "I guess she *could* have been looking at you?"

Jas instantly brightened and I kicked myself, wishing that I could be more like Lexie. She'd said it straight, and although it was hard to hear, it might have prepared Jas for not getting the role she was hoping for. All I'd done was give her more false hope.

Audition fever strikes and Jas has sparkly dreams of being a star

As our bus pulled up outside school the next morning, Jas's mobile buzzed. She grabbed it out of her bag and stared at the screen. "It's from Nisha," she said, her eyes lighting up. "Quick!"

Jas hurried off the bus and weaved through the crowds of kids on the pavement outside, with me struggling to keep up. We raced in through the gates and into the entrance foyer where a big crowd had already gathered. We fought our way through to the front beside Lexie and Nisha.

"'Auditions next Monday lunchtime'," Jas read out. "We need to prepare one of three monologues – from

either the Artful Dodger, Nancy or Oliver – and we have to sing a verse from 'Consider Yourself' or 'It's a Fine Life' or 'Where Is Love?'."

"Or, you can just sing 'Food, Glorious Food' if you audition for the chorus," Lexie added. "That's what I'm going to do!"

"Me, too. What will you pick, Jas?" Nisha asked as she read down the list.

"I think I might get all of them prepared, just in case," Jas said as she scanned the poster. "Oooh, Ellie, look! They've got a list that you can add your name to if you want to do costumes or make-up."

I glanced down and saw quite a few names on the list already. I pulled out a pen and added mine to it, feeling a mixture of excitement and nerves.

"I can't believe I'm going to be involved in a proper school production, even if it is completely offstage!" I said as Zophia added her name below mine.

"Look," Nisha pointed out, "the cast list goes up two days after! That's really quick!"

Jas rummaged through her bag and pulled out her planner, checking through it. "And rehearsals for the lead characters start next Thursday. Yup, I'm free that day!" she joked. I noticed Lexie and Nisha exchange a quick glance, like they were thinking something about Jas that they didn't want to share. It instantly made me feel protective of my BFF – I was used to her excitable ways, but I guess to them she might seem like a bit of a show-off. Luckily, Jas didn't see it, and as we all headed for registration, she was almost walking on air.

The rest of the first week back was seriously uneventful after the excitement of the auditions announcement. And all the teachers seemed to have come back from the half-term holiday on a mission to make us work even harder – even Miss Dubois was piling on the homework. Apart from PE and art, we had to do work out of school for all our subjects. Although I wasn't very good at art, I began to look forward to it more and more, especially as Miss Malik was letting us work on our entries for the Christmas card competition.

I'd decided on a picture of a robin sitting in a snowy tree, whilst Lexie was drawing Santa's sleigh flying through the air against a silhouetted backdrop. Jas had gone for an old-fashioned image of a Victorian child selling sprigs of holly in a snowy London. It didn't take a genius to work out what had inspired that! She was

eating, sleeping and dreaming *Oliver!* at the moment. Nisha had put all our efforts to shame though, with her fabulous stained-glass window collage of the three kings.

By the time the final bell of the week went after French, my homework planner was looking seriously full and I was exhausted.

"That lesson was way harder than last half term," Jas said as we grabbed our coats and headed out of the gates. "And all that homework!"

"I reckon Miss Dubois lulled us into thinking she was nice so we'd work extra hard for her," I said, thinking about the long list of vocab we'd been given to learn. "Now she's turned into a demon teacher!"

"Still, at least we've got the weekend ahead of us," said Lexie as we called goodbye to Maisie and Zophia, "and a lie-in – I can't wait!"

"Oooh! And it's Bonfire Night," Nisha said. "Fancy coming along to the display at the Sports Club? Mum and Dave, my stepdad, are taking my baby brother, Callum, so it'd be nice to have you lot to hang out with."

"Sounds good, I love fireworks!" said Lexie.

"Me, too," I added.

Stage Fright

"I'm in," Jas agreed. Suddenly her eyes lit up and she stopped in the middle of the pavement, earning a few tuts from the people walking behind. "I know! Why don't you all come to mine first, then we can practise for the audition? Ellie, you can pretend to be Mrs Crawfield and keep us all in order."

"OK!" I giggled, and Lexie and Nisha nodded.

"Great, see you at mine around four then," said Jas. "And remember to bring your singing voices!"

"Lulu, you really aren't helping," Jas sighed. Her two-year-old sister was trying to grab the hairbrush Jas was using as a microphone.

"She's just like Callum," said Nisha as Jas tried to wrestle the hairbrush away. "He always wants to do what I'm doing."

"Lulu sing!" Lulu insisted crossly. "Lulu!"

"Not right now, Lu, it's my turn," Jas told her firmly.

Lulu's lip jutted out dramatically. "Uh-oh, I've seen that face before," I said, knowing that it normally preceded a mega tantrum. Jas recognized it too, and quickly picked up a now howling Lulu and deposited her in the kitchen with her mum, Gloria.

"Right, time for the real practice to begin!" she said, shutting her bedroom door firmly. "Who wants to go first?"

"We might as well sing together," Lexie said, turning to Nisha. "We're both going to audition for the chorus and it'll be less embarrassing that way."

"Good idea!" said Nisha, "but make sure your brother doesn't come in!"

Jas checked that Josh was busy in his room playing on his Xbox, then pushed her giant beanbag up against her door. "All clear," she said, lining up "Food, glorious food" on the CD. "And … action!"

Lexie and Nisha took a deep breath, glanced across at each other, then collapsed in a fit of giggles. Jas restarted the track as they composed themselves, then they began to sing. The first couple of times it was a bit stilted, but they soon got into their stride. I hummed along with them.

"Excellent!" I cried in my best Mrs Crawfield voice as they finished the song for the fifth time. "You can both be in the chorus!"

"Are you sure you don't want to try out for the chorus, Ellie?" said Nisha as she flopped back on to the bed.

Stage Fright

I shook my head. "Definitely not," I said, blushing pink. "I'm very happy doing the behind-the-scenes stuff, thanks!"

"Right, my turn," Jas said, leaping off the bed and leafing through the *Oliver!* script that Mrs Crawfield had lent her. "I'm going to do the Artful Dodger."

I looked at her, surprised. "Don't you think that role will go to a boy?"

Jas shrugged. "Not if I do a good enough audition. And I was thinking about what Mrs Crawfield was saying about really getting into character to make it believable. I reckon I'm most like Dodger, so that'll be my best chance of giving a convincing audition."

Jas cleared her throat, looked down, then back up again, took a deep breath and began the monologue. She knew the script off by heart and brought out all the cheekiness of the character, just like Mrs Crawfield had talked about. Even though it was only me, Lexie and Nisha watching, Jas gave it her all. As she finished with a cheeky wink, we all broke into applause.

"Jas, that was awesome!" I beamed, full of admiration.

"Brilliant!" Lexie and Nisha shouted.

"Thanks, guys," Jas said, her face split by the hugest of grins.

"Now you just need to recreate that for Mrs Crawfield," said Nisha.

"Fingers crossed! Right, now for my song!"

Jas pressed play on the CD player and burst into "Consider Yourself". As soon as it finished, she scrutinized every bit of her performance and then hit the replay button. By the seventh time, her audience was becoming restless.

"I'm still not quite getting the right feeling in the first section," she said. "What do you think – one final run-through?"

"Nooo, that's enough!" Lexie groaned.

Jas looked a little hurt, but just at that moment Gloria knocked on the door. "You girls know what the time is? Nearly six o'clock! Ellie, your dad'll be here any minute to pick you up."

"Saved by the bell!" Lexie grinned. "Well, the fireworks anyway."

We bundled into Jas's narrow hallway and pulled on our outdoor gear – hats, scarves, gloves and big winter coats. The next second there was a beep from the street and we hurried outside to Dad's waiting car.

Stage Fright

"Taxi to the fireworks," Dad called as we jumped in. "So how did rehearsals go?"

"Brilliant," Jas gushed. "I so want to get the Artful Dodger!"

"That's ambitious, Jas," Dad said, frowning. "I imagine there'll be lots of people going for that role."

"It just means I have to stand out more," Jas said, confidently, "that's all."

"Well, you normally manage to ... one way or another," said Dad, winking in the mirror at Jas. I smiled, grateful to Dad for saying the right thing, as usual. Jas's own father had moved to London a few years ago, and she didn't get to see him very often. Sometimes it was like Dad had become a bit of a second father to her.

A few minutes later, we pulled into the Sports Club car park.

"I'll pick you up at nine," Dad said as we piled out. "Have fun!"

"Thanks, Dad, see you later!"

We could see the smoke from the huge bonfire rising in a swirling column into the dark sky as we made our way through the crowds. As we got closer, we could feel its searing heat and gratefully stopped

to warm ourselves up.

Once our faces were glowing we turned round until our coats felt like they might start to melt.

"I don't get how one side of you can be so hot," Lexie shivered, "and the other side freezing – you'd think the heat would seep right through!"

Suddenly, Nisha's phone beeped. "Ooh, Mum's by the food stalls," she said, reading the message. "Shall we head over?"

"Defo – I'm starving!" said Jas. We followed Nisha through the chattering crowds, stopping to say hello to some of our schoolmates. It looked like most of Priory Road was there, including Kirsty and Eliza. They were both wrapped up in matching furry hats and scarves, wearing jeggings and fluffy boots, and didn't even notice us as we hurried by. As we reached the food stalls, we caught sight of Ed next to the burger stand, holding his little sister's hand.

"Pretend you never saw this," he said. "Erase it from your memories!"

"No way," Jas giggled, quickly grabbing her phone and taking a picture. "Say cheese!"

Nisha spotted her mum and we weaved through the crowd towards her. Nisha's mum was wrapped up against the cold in a long, padded coat and she was standing next to Dave, Nisha's stepdad, who was carrying Callum on his shoulders. Nisha introduced us and we stopped and chatted for a bit.

"Hi, girls! Having a good time?" said Nisha's mum. "It's a terrific bonfire, isn't it?" She reached into her bag and pulled out a packet of sparklers. "Not too old for these, are you?" she said, smiling. We shook out heads, laughing, as she handed them round.

As they fizzed into life, we drew patterns in the air and wrote our names in huge sparkly letters. Then Jas wrote "Oliver" and swirled her sparkler round our heads.

"For good luck," she grinned.

I grinned back at her. "I'm sure you'll ace the auditions!"

We joined the queue at the hot dog stall, our teeth chattering as we waited in line. It was so cold that I could feel my nose glowing red (and Jas pointed it out!).

"I'm having mustard on mine," said Lexie as we reached the front of the queue.

"Yuck!" I grimaced. "Give me ketchup any day!"

We left Nisha's mum, Dave and Callum chatting to

friends, and made our way back to the bonfire, munching as we went.

"Hey!" said Lexie as music suddenly blared out of the speakers. "I think it's about to start!"

A moment later, the first rocket zipped into the sky and cracked into a shower of white, red and green sparkles. Two more rockets followed at once, exploding into a dazzling array of multicoloured glitter. We all stood, "ooh-ing" and "ah-ing", our breath coming out in misty clouds.

As the music built to a grand finale, the last firework shot into the air, making us jump as it exploded into a thousand sparkly colours. Everyone in the crowd gasped and cooed as they watched it slowly fade away. Soon all that was left was a faint smoky trail. I turned to see Jas still staring at the sky, her eyes shining. "I so can't wait for Monday – I hope I sparkle as brightly as that firework!"

"I'm sure you will!" said Nisha, smiling.

"And you'll probably be as loud," Lexie joked, ducking to avoid Jas's swipe.

5

The big day finally arrives...

Jas was tripping over herself with excitement from the moment I got to her gate on Monday morning.

"I didn't sleep a wink!" she said as we walked to the bus stop. "And when I did sleep, I almost wished I hadn't – I dreamed that I got up on stage with my pyjamas on…!"

"Don't worry," I giggled. "I'll make sure that doesn't happen!"

The bus arrived and we squeezed our way through to the back. Jas spent the whole journey tapping her toe, humming and fidgeting as if she had ants in her pants. "Why can't the auditions be first thing?" she said,

anxiously pulling at one of her ringlets as we arrived at school. "I bet it takes for ever to get to lunchtime."

Lexie and Nisha were waiting inside by the lockers. "You OK?" Nisha asked, noticing how jittery Jas looked.

"Absolutely," said Jas. "I just wish we could do the auditions now. And you?"

Nisha and Lexie exchanged glances and nodded, but they looked really nervous. "Come on," I said, stepping in before Jas could go through her lines one last time. "We've still got lessons to get to."

At lunchtime, Wiggy, our geography teacher, kept us all after the bell went to finish explaining the intricacies of fossilization. As he droned on, Jas looked like she was going to explode.

"Quick, run!" she cried, when he finally let us go. We raced along the corridors towards the hall, but as we rounded the last corner we were met by a line of people snaking right out of the door.

"Are we going to have to audition in front of all of them?" Nisha gulped.

"Looks like it," Lexie groaned.

Stage Fright

"I had no idea so many people would come," Jas whispered as we joined the back of the queue. For the first time since the audition poster had gone up in the foyer, she looked a bit unsure of herself. "Maybe lots of them will try out for the chorus, do you think?"

"I don't know," I replied honestly. "Maybe."

We stood on tiptoes, trying to get a glimpse inside the hall. The long line of kids led all the way up to the stage, and Mrs Crawfield was sitting at a small table in the middle, talking to one of the sixth formers. Suddenly, Mr Flight, our English teacher, appeared at the hall doors.

"Right everyone!" he called out. "It's wonderful that so many of you have turned up, but it does mean that you'll have to be patient. We're about to get started and we'll get through everyone as quickly as we can!"

There was a general nodding of heads, then he called "Good luck!" and ducked back inside.

"Are you OK?" I asked as Jas peered through the crowd, trying to see the first person up on stage. She nodded, but I could tell that she was distracted. Everyone around us was chatting, but she stayed silent, straining to hear as the boy started to speak. It was a

bit of a mumble and he broke into a smile as soon as he reached the end, looking relieved. Then he went into his song.

"His singing's way better than his monologue," Jas critiqued. "I bet he gets the chorus."

We watched as one hopeful student after another climbed up on to the stage. Tom from Kingfisher had a go, but nerves got the better of him and he forgot the words, and the tune. His friend Damon, from Goldfinch, sang really well, though. Slowly, the line in front of us grew shorter and we edged inside the hall doors. As the next few hopefuls performed their audition pieces, Jas seemed to grow a bit taller.

"I think I can hold my own with everyone so far," she whispered to me, Lexie and Nisha, just as a Year Ten girl, Amelia, stepped up on stage. She was in drama club and, from what I could tell, she was very popular. Even though she was super glamorous, she seemed genuinely friendly, unlike Kirsty and Eliza.

"When you're ready, Amelia," Mrs Crawfield called out. Amelia smiled confidently, showing dimples in each cheek, and swept back her thick brown hair. She cleared her throat, then began Nancy's monologue.

Everyone watched, completely transfixed. When she

finished she smiled again, then went straight into her song, "It's a Fine Life!".

"She's good!" Nisha whispered as she came to the end of her song and hurried off the stage.

"Amelia was the lead in last year's play, *The Boyfriend*," someone behind us said. I turned round and blushed as I realized it was a Year Eleven boy talking. He looked a bit doe-eyed, and me and Nisha exchanged glances, trying not to giggle. "I bet Mrs Crawfield casts her as Nancy."

"She can't yet, can she?" Jas said, sounding a bit panicky. "I mean, she hasn't seen everyone audition yet."

The boy laughed. "I doubt anyone will be better."

After Amelia, a string of Year Nines, Tens and Elevens stepped on and off the stage. Jas grew quieter and quieter as one after another gave brilliant auditions.

"The competition is so much stiffer than at Woodview," she whispered as another Year Eleven boy, Daniel McDonnell, took to the stage and gave a faultless performance of the Artful Dodger.

"Only two more, Jas," I said, nudging her, "then it's your turn!"

The next two both tried out for Oliver. One of them

was a Year Nine who was small, with angelic looks.

Mrs Crawfield smiled as he finished singing in a sweet voice. "Thank you, Lewis. Who's next?"

"You go up first," Jas urged Lexie, suddenly losing her nerve.

"Me?" Lexie whispered back. Jas nodded fiercely. Lexie sighed, then climbed the steps, her pony tail swinging and stood in the centre of the stage. She smiled boldly at Mr Flight and Mrs Crawfield, then burst into the chorus of "Food, Glorious Food". She rattled through it, hardly stopping to draw breath, and waited for the teachers to nod her off. She dashed down the stairs, and gave Jas a grin. "Your turn!"

Jas hesitated, then looked at Nisha. "Do you mind going next?"

Nisha shook her head. "I'd rather get it over with!" she said, hurrying up on stage.

"Are you OK?" I whispered to Jas as Nisha started to sing. Jas nodded, biting her nails, but she didn't say anything and I knew better than to ask her again. Soon Nisha had finished and she rushed back down the stairs.

"Wish me luck," Jas said, taking a deep breath.

"You can do it, Jas," I urged. Jas smiled, then started up the steps. She almost made it to the top, then tripped and flew on to the stage, just keeping upright. A few people behind us tittered and Jas beamed, taking an impromptu bow.

"When you're ready, Jasmine," Mrs Crawfield said, exchanging a glance with Mr Flight. Jas nodded, cleared her throat, and opened her mouth to speak. But nothing came out. She cleared her throat again, and stared down at everyone.

"Take your time, Jasmine," Mr Flight said. Jas looked to where I was standing and I gave her the thumbs up. She smiled, took a deep breath, then began. She started off on her short monologue for the Artful Dodger. I saw Mrs Crawfield and Mr Flight exchange a few words, looking confused.

"Maybe Josh was right," whispered Lexie. "I haven't seen any of our year auditioning for anything other than the chorus. I wonder if that's why they look a bit surprised?"

"Maybe," I said under my breath as Jas faltered for a second. But she picked it up again and carried on till the end. Then she began her song. But rather than just standing to sing, Jas acted her performance, just as she'd practised. As she finished on a long note, Mrs Crawfield nodded and thanked her. Jas stood looking

out, beaming down at everyone and enjoying her moment in the spotlight.

"Anything else?" Mr Flight asked as Jas loitered on the stage.

"Oh, no, sorry," she said, leaping down the steps.

"I'm glad that's over," Nisha sighed as we hurried out of the hall and headed for lunch.

"It was great!" said Jas. "Although I did mess up the monologue a bit."

"And now the nail-biting wait begins," Lexie said, "to find out if we make it into the cast!"

Jas groaned. "This is going to be torture!"

"Every lesson feels like it's a week long," Jas moaned as we sat in art the next day, waiting for the final bell.

"Really? Maths, maybe, but I think this lesson's whizzing by," Nisha said, her face a mask of concentration. "You lot can't have finished already, surely? Let's see."

We held up our efforts. Lexie began to giggle, then the rest of us joined in. We'd been given the task of drawing a still-life picture of a bowl of fruit, but it was harder than it looked, and apart from Nisha, we'd all pretty much given up.

Jas checked her watch. "Nearly time for drama club," she said. "I wonder if Mrs Crawfield might give us a sneaky hint about who's got which parts."

She started to pack away, whipping round and tidying everything up for the rest of us. As the bell finally buzzed, she twirled out of the room, hurrying us all along with her to the hall for drama club. But her excited anticipation was short-lived.

"I'm afraid that I can't let you into any secrets over the casting this evening," Mrs Crawfield explained. "It wouldn't be fair on any cast members who aren't part of drama club. I'm afraid you'll just have to be patient!"

Jas groaned. Patience was most definitely not one of her virtues!

The even BIGGER day arrives...!

Jas was a bundle of nerves the whole way in to school on Wednesday. As we jumped off the bus, Lexie and Nisha came running down to meet us.

"What's up?" Jas asked, frowning.

"The cast list," Lexie puffed. "That's what!"

"Have you seen it?" Jas asked, speeding up. Lexie shook her head.

"We thought it would be more fun to look together," Nisha explained.

We dodged along the pavement through the mass of maroon-and-grey blazers and in through the gates. As we headed inside the double doors, the entrance hall was buzzing with excitement. A crowd of students gathered round the poster – some were grinning and looking pleased, while others were turning away with a look of disappointment. I saw Amelia getting congratulated by lots of other Year Tens before disappearing off down the corridor, beaming.

"She must have got Nancy," Nisha guessed as we joined the throng. Jas jigged about nervously while we waited our turn to get to the front. Up ahead of us I saw Daniel whoop with joy and high-five his mates. I wondered if he'd got the Artful Dodger. If he had, where did that leave Jas's hopes for a main part?

At last we found ourselves at the front, and Nisha spotted her name.

"Chorus," she beamed.

"Me too," Lexie whooped.

"I've got backstage stuff," I said, feeling relieved. Jas was running her finger down the poster, starting at the top where all the lead roles were listed, frowning more and more. Alongside Amelia and Daniel, I noticed that Lewis had got the part of Oliver. Our Head Boy, Max, had got the part of Fagin and a large, rugby-playing sixth former, Alex, had been cast as Bill Sykes.

"I haven't got the Artful Dodger," Jas said quietly,

almost to herself. "In fact, I haven't even been given a single line to sing, not even a flower girl, or the milkmaid in the scene near the end..."

"Oh, here you are," I pointed out, suddenly spotting Jas's name.

"You're in the chorus with us!" Nisha and Lexie tried to look excited for her, but Jas couldn't hide her disappointment; her whole face drooped and her shoulders slumped.

"I guess what Josh said was true," Nisha reasoned. "There isn't a single Year Seven or Eight in any role other than the chorus."

Jas nodded, looking like she was fighting back the tears as her eyes started to glisten. "I still don't think that's fair – I worked really hard for that audition."

"I bet most people did," Lexie pointed out fairly, but Jas just pulled a face.

"Hang on a minute – look at this," said Nisha. "You're understudy for the Artful Dodger! That's brilliant, Jas!"

"Daniel's got that part, though, hasn't he?" Jas said with a bit of a waver in her voice. "So I can forget the understudy role."

"How come?" I asked, confused.

Stage Fright

"He's captain of the running squad," Lexie explained. "Probably the last person in the world to get sick."

"I might as well just give up now." She turned away and headed to the cloakroom with her head down.

"Is she always like this when she doesn't get what she wants?" Lexie asked in a whisper.

"Um, sometimes," I said, thinking about it for the first time, and suddenly feeling a bit disloyal at admitting it.

Lexie raised her eyebrows, looking less than impressed.

As we caught up with Jas at the lockers, Trin and Tabitha came up. "We're in the chorus with you!" cried Trin. "It's going to be so much fun, isn't it!"

"You reckon?" Jas asked glumly.

Lexie rolled her eyes. "Jas, at least you're in the play," she pointed out testily. "Some of our year didn't even make it that far. You should be pleased!"

Jas looked at Lexie, clearly picking up on her tone.

"I know that," she snapped back, "but I really thought I might be in with a chance, that's all."

She turned and started fiddling about with the books in her locker. Lexie and Nisha loitered for a bit, but they could see she was in a grump.

"Look, we'll see you in registration, OK?" said Lexie.

Jas nodded, but as soon as they'd disappeared and it was just the two of us, her chin began to wobble.

"I'm not being ungrateful," she sniffed, "I just thought my audition deserved more than a place in the chorus." I scrabbled around in my bag and handed her a tissue just as the first fat tear dripped off the end of her nose.

"You were just in the wrong year, that's all," I said. But in the back of my mind I wondered if Lexie had a point – maybe Jas was being a teeny bit of a diva.

She gave a big sigh and wiped her nose, trying to hide her face as Ed and Zac walked past. The next second I noticed Mrs Crawfield hurrying down the corridor. "Great," Jas groaned, "that's all I need." Mrs Crawfield looked over and smiled at me, then peered towards Jas, faltered, and stopped right in front of us.

"Everything all right?" she asked, catching sight of Jas's red eyes. Jas nodded. Then her face crumpled again.

"Well, not really," she sniffed. "I … I really wanted to play the Artful Dodger, or … or at least get some kind of solo in the play. I practised like mad for the audition."

"I could see that, Jas," Mrs Crawfield said matter-of-factly, "and you showed great promise at the audition, but there were more polished performances than yours on the day. Don't forget, you were auditioning with children who have a lot more experience than you, so the competition is bound to be a lot tougher than you're used to."

Jas sighed. "I guess."

"And you may not know this," the teacher continued, "but you're the only Year Seven ever to have been given an understudy role, which demonstrates how much faith I have in your talents. Now, chin up, get to registration and I'll see you for chorus rehearsals next week! Deal?"

Jas nodded, trying to smile, but as Mrs Crawfield floated off down the corridor, Jas's eyes watered again. "I still think it's unfair," she mumbled.

Miss Dubois looked up questioningly as we walked in halfway through registration. She could tell that Jas was upset, and asked her to stay behind.

I waited outside with Lexie and Nisha.

"Ooh, Ellie," Lexie said, glancing towards the door and lowering her voice. "There's something me and Nisha wanted to ask you."

I frowned. "What?"

"We wondered if you fancied meeting up in town in

a couple of weekends' time?" Lexie continued. "Only, it has to be without Jas!"

"Without Jas?" I squeaked, feeling suddenly wrong-footed "How come?"

Nisha smiled. "So we can buy her birthday present, that's all!"

I grinned with relief. "Ooooh, yes! Great idea!"

Suddenly we heard voices on the other side of the door and quickly stepped apart, looking shifty.

"You know where I am if you want to talk, Jas, *oui*?" Miss Dubois said as she held the door open for Jas.

"Um-hm," Jas replied. Miss Dubois smiled at the rest of us and disappeared down the corridor.

"What did she say?" I asked as soon as she'd gone.

"She just wanted to know why I was upset." Jas sighed. "She was really sweet about it, but that still doesn't get me a solo in the play, does it?"

Lexie rolled her eyes without trying to hide it.

"Anyway, what were you all whispering about before I came out?" Jas asked.

I looked at Lexie and Nisha, opening and closing my mouth like a goldfish. "Oh, we were, um, just saying…"

"…that we should go down to the diner after school," Nisha jumped in. "To celebrate all of us getting a part in the play."

"I don't know," Jas said, still looking at us a bit suspiciously. "It's a nice idea, but I'm not sure I'm in the mood."

I was about to say something, knowing that all it would take to get Jas out of the dumps was a bit of an ego boost, but Lexie beat me to it. And clearly she wasn't into humouring Jas.

"Well, suit yourself," she said. "But we're going."

"Fine, so you won't miss me if I don't come, then," Jas replied tartly, before stomping off down the corridor.

The three of us exchanged glances. "Remember we made a pact not to fall out this term," Nisha said, looking pointedly at Lexie. "So stop rubbing Jas up the wrong way – she's clearly upset."

"I'm just saying it like it is," Lexie protested. "And she's making out like it's a failure to be in the chorus – she doesn't seem to realize that for some of us that's a real achievement!"

"I'll talk to her," I said, desperate to smooth things over. Lexie had a point, but after the horrors of the first half term I didn't want Jas to think we were singling her out; I knew how that felt only too well.

Jas was in a huff for the rest of the morning, but at lunchtime I had a chance to talk to her. Miss Malik had given Nisha permission to work on her Christmas card design and Lexie had cross-country practice following Terrifying Townsend picking her for the team. Lexie hadn't been at all keen, but she'd been even less keen to say "no" to Terrifying Townsend.

We found a free table in the corner of the dining hall and sat down at one end. "Is everything all right?" I asked as Jas prodded at her spaghetti. I could feel the tension even between us two.

"I guess," Jas said. "Lexie just bugged me this morning. She can be so opinionated sometimes."

I looked at Jas, my eyebrows disappearing under my fringe.

"What?" she asked.

"Er, you can talk," I said, laughing. "Maybe that's why you two clash a bit sometimes ... you're both pretty strong willed."

Jas tried hard not to smile.

"And I think she just wants you to be pleased that we're all going to be in the play together – I know you

68

haven't got the part you were hoping for, but Mrs Crawfield knows how brilliant you are, otherwise she wouldn't have given you the understudy role. And we can still have lots of fun, right?"

That did the trick. Jas's face cracked into a grin. "OK, OK, I'll try. Just quit the big pleading eyes!"

"Great!" I beamed. "Listen, about tonight: are you one hundred per cent sure that you're not in the mood for a strawberry shake? Or even one of Joey's world-famous hot chocolates?" I could see that Jas was beginning to waver. "With a sprinkling of miniature marshmallows?"

"Ooh, all right then," she said. "Maybe I could be persuaded!"

Jas was fine again with Lexie during the afternoon, and it was almost as if she had forgotten all about the play. But as we headed out of the school gates we bumped into Josh heading for the bus stop.

"Ugh, I bet he says I told you so about *Oliver!*," Jas grumbled, suddenly looking downcast again.

"Hey sis, you all right?" he said, looking concerned. "I saw you got the chorus. You OK about it?"

Jas shrugged and Josh nudged her arm. "I know you wanted a bigger part, but it'll be fun. Trust me, I've been there. You off into town?"

Jas glanced up, looking wrong-footed by Josh's niceness. She nodded.

"I'll let Mum know you'll be a bit late," he said. "Catch you later."

He dashed across the road to the bus stop, leaving Jas staring after him.

"Wonders never cease," she said, looking secretly pleased.

"Not a single gloat in sight," I agreed as we headed off into town.

Joey looked up and smiled as we entered the diner, holding out his arms like we were long-lost friends. Well, I guess it had been at least two weeks since we'd last been in.

"Now, I'm guessing in this chilly weather that milkshakes made with ice cream may not be what you guys need. Am I right or am I right?" he asked, raising one eyebrow. "So, what are we talking – hot chocolates? Marshmallows? Flakes?"

"The works, please! Times four!" Lexie said, rubbing her nose to warm it up. We fished out our money and Joey waved us over to our favourite table, saying he'd bring the drinks.

A few moments later, the tall glasses arrived overflowing with tiny pink and white melting marshmallows and chocolate flakes. "Wow!" Nisha gasped. "These look seriously amazing."

"Amazing enough to banish all disappointments in life," I added, taking a sip and getting froth all over my lips.

"Like Wiggy DJing at our junior disco," Lexie said, raising her glass and taking a gulp. "Er, scratch that, not even hot chocolate this good can banish that disappointment!"

We all giggled. "This half term is turning into a bit of a disaster," Jas sighed, sipping her drink.

"No, it isn't, Jas," I said firmly. "Last half term was a total disaster. Nothing that bad's happened."

"Yet," Lexie added cheekily.

"And we've still got your birthday to look forward to," I said as Lexie and Nisha both grinned at me. I couldn't keep from cracking a smile, either.

"What's so funny?" Jas asked.

"Nothing," I said, concentrating on my hot chocolate.

"And there's your party," said Lexie, quickly changing the subject.

"Ooh, yes," I said. "Your skating party is going to be awesome."

"And don't forget Christmas!" Nisha added.

"OK, OK," Jas said, half smiling. She took a sip and looked wistfully out of the window, but as I caught sight of her large brown eyes in the reflection, I wasn't sure that she was entirely convinced.

On Thursday morning Miss Dubois pulled Jas to one side and explained that Mrs Crawfield wanted her to attend all the rehearsals, so that she could learn the understudy role for Dodger. It was as if a light had gone on in Jas's head and suddenly she was enthusiastic about the play again.

That evening, as I sat curled up on the sofa with Crumble, I texted Jas.

Hey Jas, how was ur rehearsal? x

She replied straight away.

Stage Fright

Gr8! Can't wait 2 get up on stage nxt wk! ☺ x

Dad looked over at the sound of my text message alert.

"Anything interesting?" he asked.

I nodded, smiling. "Jas – she seems happy about the play again, thank goodness. I just hope she stays that way – she's hard work when she's grumpy!"

Jas gets frustrated, then comes up with the most Jas-genius idea (according to her...)

The weekend whizzed by, filled with homework, homework and more homework. I went round to Jas's on Sunday afternoon to watch a DVD, but all she wanted to do was learn her lines in case Daniel just happened to sprain his ankle and she had to take to the stage. After the last bell on Tuesday we all raced to the hall for the first chorus rehearsal. Jas bounced in, all enthusiastic from Thursaday's rehearsal, but her mood drooped pretty much straight away.

"Mrs Crawfield hasn't even bothered to turn up to direct the chorus!" she groaned, as Mr Flight called everyone to attention. "This is just getting worse!"

Stage Fright

I noticed Damon from our year shoot her a disapproving look, but Jas was too wrapped up in her own grump to notice.

"You could at least give him a chance," Lexie said. "He might be really good."

Jas looked doubtful.

"Right, before we begin, Mrs Crawfield has prepared a rehearsal schedule. Please take one and pass them on," said Mr Flight. "There are lots of extra rehearsals after school, so I hope you'll all be able to make them."

As we each took a schedule, a girl with a long auburn plait called out, "Can those of you who signed up to do make-up and costumes come over to this corner, please?"

"I'll see you in a bit," I said, feeling relieved to have an excuse to leave Jas. "Try and have fun!" I said, giving her my most cheery smile.

I split off and stood in a huddle with Maisie, Molly and Zophia from my form and Georgie from Peregrine.

"I've never done anything like this before!" Georgie whispered nervously.

"Me neither!" I said. In between listening to the auburn-haired girl, Abbie, explaining what we'd be

doing, I glanced over at the stage.

"First we're going to run through 'Food, glorious food!'." I heard Mr Flight announce. "We'll start off down here, then we'll move on to the stage and walk through where everyone will stand once we're word perfect."

Mr Flight handed round the music and Mr Thomas, the music teacher, began to play the piano. As the chorus started to sing, Jas's voice sounded out loud and clear above all the others.

"OK, we're going to split you into two teams," Abbie said, grabbing my attention back again. "Those of you who want to do costumes stand over here with me, and those of you who want to specialize in make-up, stand with Claire."

I hesitated for a second, unsure which I wanted to try. In the end I thought that learning how to apply make-up might come in handy, especially after my mascara disaster last half term, so I headed over to Claire, along with Georgie. Claire ran through the basics of what kind of stage make-up we'd be using, and with the help of a volunteer she showed us some of the techniques. As I watched and listened I suddenly realized that I was fizzing with excitement! It was amazing to be part of it all. After we'd finished, I stayed behind with a couple of others who had friends in the chorus, too.

"Now, can all the tall people move to the back please," Mr Flight called out, "and let's have the smaller ones at the front."

I saw Jas's disappointed face – she was one of the tallest and she was soon shifted from the front of the stage to the back. She didn't make a fuss, but as the rehearsal came to an end she hurried over with Lexie and Nisha.

"That was such good fun, but I *hate* being stuck at the back," she grumbled. "I can't believe that not only have I been overlooked for a star role, but I've been stuck out of sight, too!"

"All the tall people had to move to the back, Jas," Lexie said, with a sigh, "not just you."

"I know that, Lexie," Jas bristled, "I was just saying it was annoying, that was all."

"That's not the only thing," Lexie muttered.

"What's that supposed to mean?" Jas demanded.

"Just that some of us are happy in the chorus, and if you were, too, we all might enjoy it more," Lexie snapped. Jas's face turned stony. We walked through

the empty corridors in heavy silence, fetched our coats then headed into the dark, drizzling evening.

"It sounds like Molly's going to be a great help with the costumes," I said, desperate to break the silence. "Her nan's a seamstress and she already knows how to use a sewing machine. Abbie, who's looking after the costumes, reckons she's a natural."

"Just goes to show that Years Seven and Eight are talented, too," Jas said pointedly. "It's not just the older years who are good at stuff, like Mrs Crawfield seems to think." Suddenly she stopped, her face lighting up. "That's it! I can't believe I didn't think of this before!"

"What?" we all asked.

"A talent show! We could hold one at Priory Road!" Jas exclaimed. "That would show Mrs Crawfield that we're every bit as talented as anyone else in the school! It'll give everyone who was disappointed not to get a part in *Oliver!* a chance to step into the spotlight after all!"

Our bus appeared in the distance. Me, Nisha and Lexie exchanged glances. "Do you reckon lots of people were disappointed, then?" Lexie asked.

Jas shrugged. "I'll guess we'll find out," she replied coolly, obviously still smarting from Lexie's earlier comment. "See you tomorrow."

Stage Fright

Jas linked arms with me and we raced across the road and on to the bus. She hurried upstairs and I stopped to wave at Lexie and Nisha – from the looks on their faces they didn't seem quite as keen on Jas's idea as she did.

On Wednesday, Jas wasted no time spreading the word about the talent show. As soon as we got to class she jumped on to her chair and whistled to get everyone's attention.

"What does everyone think about having a Years Seven and Eight talent show?" Jas asked. "Who'd be up for it?"

"What, like *Britain's Got Talent*?" Zac piped up.

Jas nodded.

"Who'll be the judges?" Ajay asked.

"Well, me, I guess," Jas frowned, "and my mates." I felt myself blush as Tom and Jordan immediately shook their heads, muttering "No way". Jas ignored them and carried on. "I haven't thought out all the details yet."

"Have the teachers agreed?" Travis asked.

"If we get enough interest they'll have to," Jas smiled.

I glanced round. Some of the class were looking at each other, keen to hear more. Others, including Kirsty, clearly couldn't have cared less. In front of us, Nisha and Lexie had turned round in their seats, but whereas Nisha looked enthusiastic, Lexie seemed very subdued.

"I'm up for it!" Ed called out.

"Yeah, and me," Zac joked.

"You could belly dance," Ed guffawed, earning a thump from Zac just as the door opened. Jas quickly leaped off her chair and sat down.

Miss Dubois took the register and, as we left the room to get to geography, Jas called out, "Let me know if you're interested and spread the word!"

Jas's enthusiasm was pretty infectious, and by the end of lunchtime she had quite a list of people who wanted to take part, including some Year Eights.

"So what happens now?" Lexie asked.

"I'm going to go and talk to Mrs Crawfield," Jas said confidently. "And tell her how many people want to take part."

"Then what?" I asked.

"Then I get my opportunity to shine after all!" Jas beamed.

"You want to be in it, too?" said Lexie, looking

surprised. "But who's going to organize it all?"

"We will, of course!" said Jas. The three of us didn't look convinced. "Come on, it won't exactly take much doing, will it? It's just getting a bunch of people to turn up in the hall and perform their act, that's all."

Nisha looked worried. "Are you sure that's all there is to it? Will we be needed at lunchtimes? It's just that I've offered to help Miss Malik with painting the set for *Oliver!* so I'm going to be pretty busy."

"And I'll have cross-country training some lunchtimes," Lexie added.

"And we've still got the play to fit in, don't forget," I said, as we headed to the staffroom.

"Well, I'll organize it by myself if I have to, alongside the play," Jas said, sounding a bit let down.

She raced ahead of us and knocked on the door. We hovered in the background while Jas talked to Mrs Crawfield. After a couple of minutes, Mrs Crawfield frowned, disappeared into the staffroom, and returned a moment later with Miss Dubois. After much nodding and chatting Jas turned and walked over to us, grinning from ear to ear.

"They said yes!" she beamed. "Mrs Crawfield told me that I couldn't do it on my own, so she'd only agree

if Miss Dubois said she'd help. She was a bit unsure about it, but once I promised that I'd work really hard, she gave in and agreed!"

"Was Mrs Crawfield cross?" I asked, remembering the look on her face.

"Um, a bit," Jas said dismissively. "She said she thought she'd explained the situation, and that it wasn't to do with lack of talent – just experience. Anyway, I said that you guys might be able to help out a bit, too, if you're not too busy."

"Of course I'll help," I said, feeling bad that I hadn't been more enthusiastic. "It's just that if it takes up lots of time I might not be able to help with all of it…"

"And me," Nisha and Lexie said together.

"Excellent!" Jas grinned. "I mean, who wouldn't want to be involved with the best talent show Priory Road has ever seen?"

I smiled – when Jas was all excited about something it was hard not to get excited too.

"So, how do we even begin?" Nisha asked, looking a bit overwhelmed.

"Miss Dubois suggested that we have a meeting with her tomorrow lunchtime to go through all the details. And she told me to make a poster to advertize the show and the auditions. I'll do that tonight after rehearsals. Miss Dubois said that we can hold our auditions on Monday lunchtime in the hall."

"I can't do Monday lunchtime," Lexie pointed out, "I've got cross-country training."

Jas made a bit of a face. "Wouldn't you rather do this?" she asked. "It'll be more fun."

"Try telling Terrifying Townsend that!" Lexie replied.

"Well, OK," Jas said, trying not to look too bothered. "So it'll just be us three on the judging panel, then!"

Nisha and I smiled, but inside I felt my stomach flip. It was clear Jas and Lexie were still cross with each other, and Jas had just made it worse by making Lexie feel left out. And on top of this, we now had a talent show to put on! Even with Miss Dubois on board, I had no idea how it would all come together, and by the looks of it, neither did Jas!

Miss Dubois and Mrs Crawfield are less than impressed...

The next *Oliver!* rehearsal was also focused on the chorus. They had a lot of songs and Mrs Crawfield wanted them note-perfect. I sat at the back with Claire and the rest of the make-up team – Claire had laid out the contents of the make-up cupboard and we started off by sorting through the stage paints, and seeing what had dried up and what was usable. Then we began thinking about the make-up for the different characters, starting with Fagin's gang. They were a bunch of urchins, so Claire suggested giving them pale faces with patches of dirt. Whenever I glanced up I could see Jas looking restless as Mrs Crawfield, Mr Flight and Mr Thomas ran through one of the songs for the umpteenth time. And on a couple of occasions Mrs Crawfield told her off for not concentrating and being in the wrong position onstage.

As the rehearsal ended, Mrs Crawfield clapped her hands. "Thank you, everyone," she said loudly. "See you at the next rehearsal on Monday evening, where I expect everyone's full attention, and that includes you, Jasmine, because we'll be joining the chorus up with the lead roles for the first time."

I felt myself blush on Jas's behalf, but she didn't seem at all perturbed at being singled out.

She jumped off the stage with Lexie and Nisha and they hurried over to meet me as I finished putting away the last of the make-up. "Will you be doing our make-up?" Nisha asked.

"I don't know," I said, "but I hope so!"

As we grabbed our coats and headed outside, Jas danced along in front of us. "I couldn't concentrate at all!" she said breathlessly. "I had so much stuff about the talent show spinning round in my head. There's so much to organize, I'm going to make a list tonight! As well as the posters, of course."

"Hey, Jas, wait for me!" I yelled as I leaped off the bus the following morning and charged after her, careering into several people in the process.

"Sorry, Ellie, I just want to put up these posters for the talent show before registration," she said, delving into her bag and pulling out two slightly crumpled sheets of paper. She hurried into school and put one up in the foyer and the other by the Year Seven lockers.

Priory Road Talent Show!

*Calling all mega-talented Year Sevens & Eights —
this is your time to shine!
All acts welcome — auditions to be held Monday
lunchtime in the hall.*

She had decorated the posters with stars, and as soon as the first one was up, kids started to buzz around it. Jas grinned as we headed to registration and she was on a high all morning. Even a telling-off from Miss Malik in art didn't wipe the smile off her face.

Stage Fright

When the bell went for lunchtime, she jumped up, grabbing her bag. "I guess we better go and meet Miss Dubois to start organizing the talent show," she said. We headed back to our classroom, with Jas striding ahead. Miss Dubois was already there, cleaning the whiteboard from the last lesson.

"Hello, girls," she smiled, grabbing a pen and paper and sitting down opposite us. "I've seen the poster – it looks great. Now we just have to work out how the show is going to run, *oui*? What have you planned so far?" We all looked at Jas expectantly.

"Right," Jas said, pulling out her notebook. She kept it tilted up so that Miss Dubois couldn't see the pages. I could, though, and all it contained were a load of doodles decorating the words "talent show", "audition", "a chance to shine!". "Um, so, auditions on Monday, like the poster says. Um, I haven't got much further than that really … I was just going to see who turned up and, er…"

Jas trailed off and Miss Dubois raised a perfectly shaped eyebrow. "Have you not thought about how many acts you want in the final show?" she asked. "Or when the final will be held? What about rehearsals – how many do you think you might need, when will you

hold them – and where will you hold them? And who do you want to invite for the audience – will it be for the rest of the school, or do you want parents to come?"

Miss Dubois paused for a moment, looking round at us. I felt myself going pink as Jas furiously made notes.

"*D'accord*, I think you have a lot to think about over the weekend, Jas," Miss Dubois said, standing up and getting ready to leave. "And remember, I agreed to help out, but this is your idea and it is down to you to make it a success, *oui*?"

Jas nodded and thanked Miss Dubois, then we headed to the dining hall.

"I had no idea it would be so complicated," Jas admitted, as we joined the queue.

"Or so much work," Nisha said quietly.

"There's so much practical stuff," Lexie agreed.

"Thank goodness Miss Dubois agreed to help," I said. "Without her, we'd never get this off the ground!"

On Saturday afternoon, Jas popped round to mine to do a bit of talent show planning before we headed into town to watch the turning-on of the town's Christmas lights.

"So have you got the list of things Miss Dubois said to think about?" I asked, as we went up to my room, with Crumble in hot pursuit.

"Yup," she said, collapsing on the bed and pulling her notebook out of her bag. "Well, kind of," she admitted. I glanced at the open page, but instead of answers to Miss Dubois's questions, there was a different kind of list, decorated with butterflies and question marks.

"What's all that?" I asked, pointing to it.

"Oh, I was just thinking about what act I could do at the talent show," Jas grinned.

"Are you sure you're going to have time to take part *and* organize the show?" I asked. "Aren't you going to be busy enough?"

Jas shrugged. "It'll be fine," she said dismissively. "I mean, the reason I had the idea of the talent show in the first place was so that I could step into the spotlight after losing out on a lead role in *Oliver!*. I know it's really good that we can show off other people's talents, but I love being on stage as well, and I've got *so* many ideas for what I could perform."

I bit my lip, wondering whether to say anything, but I didn't push it. Instead we spent the next half-hour discussing Jas's options for her slot at the talent show. By the time we headed into town, we hadn't answered a single one of Miss Dubois's questions.

We hold auditions and Jas gets singled out – not in a good way...

"Do you think this is everyone?" Jas asked, looking round the hall on Monday lunchtime. Me and Nisha had dragged a table into the middle, facing the stage, and fetched three chairs. Now we were sitting down, clutching our notepads and wondering what to do next. I'd felt really excited and important when we'd first arrived, but as I glanced round at the crowd of people, that feeling started to evaporate.

A few people wandered over.

"So what do we do now we're here, then?" a Year Eight girl carrying a flute asked.

"Um, go up on stage I guess," Jas suggested,

looking a bit flummoxed.

"What, everyone?" a boy carrying a football asked, looking confused.

"I guess you need to form a line," I said, going bright pink as everyone looked at me, "and go up one by one."

"Good idea, Ellie." Jas smiled. Then she turned round, stood on her chair and called out at the top of her voice. "Can everyone get into a line and then we'll call you up on to the stage one at a time to perform your act."

"Are you three going to judge us?" another Year Eight called out.

"Er, yes," Jas replied.

"Forget that." A crowd of Year Eights left the line and headed for the door.

"We aren't going to have many to choose from at this rate," Nisha whispered to me under her breath.

"Can we get on with it?" Jason from Goldfinch asked. "I've got a guitar lesson in ten minutes."

"Yes, let's get started," Jas agreed, sounding a bit flustered. "Do you want to go first, then?"

"Hang on," the girl with the flute protested, "I was here before him!"

Stage Fright

As a few acts started to climb on to the stage at once, I turned to see a whole load of people heading in through the doors. Suddenly the hall seemed packed. "What have we let ourselves in for?" I squeaked, elbowing Nisha.

"I think Lexie had a lucky escape," she agreed, just as someone clapped their hands. We all turned to see Miss Dubois make her way to the front and climb the steps to the stage. She gave us a bit of a look, then waited for everyone to stop talking.

"Everyone off the stage," she said firmly, "and form a line on the right-hand side. As soon as there's a bit of order in here we'll be ready to begin the auditions."

She clacked back down the stairs and Nisha fetched her a chair. She sat down, leaned forward and looked questioningly at Jas. "How long does each act have?"

"Oh, I hadn't thought…" Jas trailed off as she saw Miss Dubois's face. "Um, five minutes?"

"Far too long," Miss Dubois replied quickly. "I'd suggest thirty seconds if it's poor, a minute if it's promising. One of you keep an eye on the time, please."

"I'll do that," I offered, glad of something to do.

"Let's have the first act!" Miss Dubois called out.

Then she turned to Jas. "Over to you."

"Um, begin, please!" Jas called out.

"Ask them their name and their form first, so you can make a note," Miss Dubois whispered to her. "Otherwise how will you know who is who, and who to ask to be in the talent show?"

"Right," Jas said, getting confused. Then, just as the girl with the flute began, Jas butted in, calling out, "Name, please?"

The girl stopped and rolled her eyes. "Forget it! If it's this disorganized it'll be a disaster!"

"Um, next!" Jas called out as the girl slammed the door and another couple of acts trailed out after her. Jas gulped, looking upset.

As the auditions finally got underway I tried to give each act my full attention. Some of them were pretty awful; Sam from our class tried to do some magic, only he dropped all his cards; then Miles from Year Eight tried to tell some jokes, but forgot all the punchlines, and a girl from Peregrine who I'd never seen before attempted to juggle five balls and dropped the lot.

After the juggler, Ed appeared at the front of the queue and we all groaned, but he actually did some pretty funny impressions of all the teachers. Miss

Dubois wasn't entirely sure, but the rest of the hall was in stitches, and after that it got better and better. I looked across at Jas's notepad, where she was writing each act's name. Next to each one there was a tick in the "good" column and a couple in the "ace" column next to it. One of the last acts to audition was Ajay, Travis and Dev who, it turned out, played in a band. They played a cover of "Love is Everything", but none of them sang.

"Don't you have a vocalist?" Jas called out.

"Well, we have," Ajay replied. "Only problem is, she goes to another school, so it's just us three for this."

"Pity," Jas said. "You're really good."

Finally we were down to the last act, a girl called Melissa, who did a hula-hoop performance.

"Brilliant!" Jas called out as I held up my hand to indicate a minute was up. As Melissa caught her hoops, Jas added, "We'll let you know, thanks!"

"*Trés bien*, that was a very good turnout," Miss Dubois said, standing up. "You clearly spotted a gap that needed to be filled! Now you have to decide who goes through to the show. Then you have to let them know, *d'accord*?"

"OK," Jas said. The three of us exchanged a quick

glance as Miss Dubois left.

"That bit's going to be so hard!" I said. "I'd hate to have to tell someone they haven't got through!"

"Me too," Nisha agreed.

"Don't remind me!" said Jas as we headed to the dining hall. Lexie was already at the table, looking red-faced after cross country. She waved us over and we plonked ourselves down.

"That was so much fun!" said Jas, beaming from ear to ear. "Why don't we go to the diner after school tonight? That way we can go through all the acts and decide which ones to axe and which to keep!"

"We've got *Oliver!* rehearsals tonight, Jas. We can't miss them," I pointed out. Jas's face clouded.

"We could skip it just this once," she suggested. "This is way more exciting. And we can go through our own acts, too!"

"I'm with Ellie – I don't want to miss any rehearsals," Lexie said firmly. "I think they're exciting. And anyway, I don't think I'll be doing an act for the talent show. I'm way too busy."

Jas shot Lexie an exasperated look. "Really?" she said. Lexie nodded.

"Me too," Nisha said quietly.

Stage Fright

Jas looked a bit miffed that our enthusiasm for the talent show wasn't as all-consuming as hers. "Well, there's bound to be a bit of hanging around during rehearsals," she said grumpily, "so I guess I'll have to go through the acts then … on my own," she added pointedly.

"Jas," Lexie said, sounding frustrated, "we can't just skip *Oliver!* rehearsals because it suits you – we'll be chucked out!"

"Whatever!" Jas huffed, shoving the piece of paper in her bag and focusing on her baked potato.

As we headed to lessons after lunch, Lexie was still annoyed. "She's being such a diva!" she said as we followed behind her.

Nisha bit her lip and glanced at me, clearly hoping I'd be able to smooth things over.

"She's just a bit one-track minded at the moment, that's all," I explained, going into autopilot and defending Jas as usual.

"*Way* more than a bit," Lexie muttered. "It's getting seriously annoying."

"I'll have a word with her," I said hurriedly.

Someone did have a word with Jas, but it wasn't me. At rehearsals that evening I was at the back of the hall, with Claire, Georgie and the rest of the make-up gang. I had my back to the stage so couldn't see what was going on, but suddenly I noticed Claire frowning.

"That's your friend, isn't it?" she asked, nodding in the direction of the stage. I followed her gaze and saw Jas standing towards the back of the chorus group, staring at a piece of paper in her hand, rather than listening to Mr Flight's instructions as they ran through "It's a Fine Life". Only Jas hadn't noticed that Mrs Crawfield was watching from the other side of the hall. As I wondered what on earth I could do, Mrs Crawfield started to advance up the steps, then called the chorus to a halt.

"Jasmine Cole," she said, loud enough for us to hear at the back.

Claire shook her head. "Uh-oh, someone's in trouble."

I watched as Mrs Crawfield asked her to explain what she was doing. Jas squirmed, but there was no point in pretending.

"I was just trying to go through the acts," Jas said sheepishly, "for the talent show..."

Stage Fright

"Then I suggest you do so elsewhere," Mrs Crawfield said sternly, "so you don't disturb everyone else. And as your heart doesn't seem to be in *Oliver!*, you are no longer needed in the chorus."

"What? But I really want to be in the play!" Jas said desperately. "I won't do it again, I promise!"

"You should have thought of that before you took on the talent show," Mrs Crawfield said coolly. "It's not up for discussion. Now, we need to continue the rehearsal, so please leave the stage."

Jas looked seriously embarrassed as the rest of the chorus parted and she stepped quickly to the front of the stage and hopped down the steps. I saw Lexie and Nisha make a face at each other as Jas headed over towards where I was sitting.

"I guess I better make sure that the talent show is the best ever now," she said. Her voice was shaky, but she forced a smile as the singing started up again.

"Maybe Mrs Crawfield is right," I said tentatively. "I mean, there's loads of stuff to do for the show."

Jas nodded. "And at least I can have a starring role in that," she added, sounding falsely cheerful about it. "Anyway, no point hanging around here. Will you be all right getting the bus alone?"

"I might call Dad and see if he can collect me," I said, not keen on the idea of getting the bus on my own in the dark. "Are you sure you don't want to wait for a lift?"

"No, I think I'll get going." Jas's eyes were glistening as she turned to go and I knew that she was really hurt. I wanted to follow her out, but Claire gave a little cough, reminding me that I still had stuff to do.

That evening I was on the computer researching some history homework, when an instant message popped up. It was from Nisha to Jas, me and Lexie.

You ok Jas? Bit rubbish getting kicked off the play...

I waited for a moment, then saw a reply ping up from Jas.

I'm ok thx

Really? I wrote quickly.

Stage Fright

Oh *sigh* maybe just a bit gutted, but guess I was pretty rude...?

Just a bit lol Lexie replied.

R u guys going 2 stay in the play, or do u fancy boycotting it in protest n helping with the show instead...?

Play 4 me, Jas, Nx Nisha replied.

& me Lexie replied.

The next message was just sent to me.

How about you, Els?

Sorry Jas, loving the play – can't give it up! But will help all I can with the show.

"Sounds like lots of activity," said Dad, as he sat on the sofa reading the paper, listening to the messages pinging backwards and forwards. "Everything all right?"

"I'm not sure, Dad," I said. I explained to him about

Jas being kicked out of the chorus and how things were a bit tense between us because all she could think about was the talent show.

"Trouble is, Jas is used to me going along with her plans. But Lexie's opened my eyes to that a bit – I mean, I don't have to agree with her all the time, do I?"

"Course not," Dad said, getting up and ruffling my hair. "You're your own person, Shrimp – don't forget that."

"I know," I sighed, "but I reckon it's going to be difficult getting Jas to understand that."

I checked my messages one last time before I headed to bed, but Jas hadn't sent a reply.

Talent show trauma and Jas starts to get suspicious as a secret mission is planned...

On Tuesday morning, Jas disappeared straight up to the art room to get some coloured art paper for framing her new talent show poster. While she was gone, me, Lexie and Nisha huddled together to make plans for her birthday.

"Are you still on for going present shopping this weekend?" I asked.

"Yup, definitely," Nisha said.

"Have you got any ideas of what to get her?" Lexie asked.

"Well, I know that Jas is getting a karaoke machine from her mum, Josh and Lulu," I said, "so maybe we

could get her some DVDs for it?"

"That's such a cool idea!" Nisha beamed.

"It's perfect! Then she can be the biggest diva any time she wants!" Lexie giggled, just as Jas reappeared. As the three of us sprang apart, we looked at each other, wondering if Jas had heard anything. If she had, she pretended not to notice and just stuck up the poster:

Priory Road Talent Show!

All acts passed the judging panel —
everyone welcome at the talent show!
Rehearsals begin at lunchtime on Wednesday.
See you there!

"Hang on a sec, you put all the acts through?" Lexie asked, looking surprised.

"I thought about it very carefully," Jas said, immediately on the defensive. "But I didn't want anyone to feel left out or let down so in the end I decided to keep everyone in."

Stage Fright

"What, even Sam, the terrible magician who fluffed his tricks?" I asked.

"And Miles, who couldn't remember any of his jokes?" Nisha said, frowning.

"Or that juggler you told me about – who dropped all her balls!" Lexie said, giggling as she remembered.

We all looked at Jas in amazement.

"OK, OK – so Lulu trashed my list!" she confessed. "She didn't mean to – she wanted to make Christmas decorations and used that bit of paper to practise with. There wasn't much left afterwards, just loads of tiny scraps, so I thought I'd just put everyone through. Anyway, the first rehearsal's tomorrow lunchtime. Are you all free?"

"Sorry, Jas, I'm helping Miss Malik with the scenery," Nisha said, looking slightly awkward.

"I can't make it, either," said Lexie, "I've got another cross-country meeting."

"OK, fine," Jas said dismissively.

"We did tell you we had other stuff on from the start," Lexie explained a bit testily.

"Yeah, I know," Jas said calmly. She turned to me and I noticed that she looked a bit uncertain. "Ellie?"

"Course," I agreed. Jas gave a small smile, then

strode ahead to registration.

"Do you think she heard us?" I whispered, feeling anxious. As Nisha and Lexie leaned in to reply, Jas suddenly turned round and caught us again – all huddled together with guilty looks on our faces.

I tried to be the best BFF ever after that – the last thing Jas needed was to think we were ganging up on her. Whenever we were on our own I brought up the talent show, telling Jas how much I was looking forward to it, and discussing the acts, and what she might do. And as we raced into the hall on Wednesday lunchtime for the first rehearsal, I was feeling excited, too. But as soon as I saw how many people had turned up I had an attack of jittery nerves.

"Quick, let's set up the table," Jas suggested as the noise levels grew. A couple of the musical acts started to warm up and tune their instruments.

"So what do we do with everyone?" I asked, looking round anxiously.

"Um, I ... I didn't think that far ahead," Jas said, biting her lip.

I glanced at the door, hoping that Miss Dubois

would come to our rescue once more. Seconds later, I felt a wave of relief as the doors swung open. But no sooner had I danced for joy than my heart leaped into my mouth. Behind her was Terrifying Townsend.

"WHAT IS ALL THIS NOISE?!" she yelled at the top of her voice. "SILENCE!"

The hall fell silent in a second. Miss Dubois turned to her calmly. "I'll take it from here, thank you, Mrs Townsend. I know you have children waiting for you outside."

Terrifying Townsend glowered over towards me and Jas, making me go pink, before stomping back out of the doors, muttering something about letting us all run riot.

Miss Dubois hurried over, her eyebrows raised. "It takes a lot to keep everything under control, *oui*?" she said. We both nodded. "So, what is your plan for the rehearsal, Jas?"

"Well, we kind of don't have one," Jas said. "Only that everyone would turn up and, um, there'd be a rehearsal."

Miss Dubois had only ever looked cheery up to this point, but right now she looked scarily stony-faced. "But I gave you a list of things to think about, *non*?"

Jas nodded. "Well, what have you done with it?"

"Er, not that much yet," Jas said lamely, "but I was planning to—"

"Well, your planning is a little late," Miss Dubois said crossly as she stepped to the front and addressed the acts. "Right, I'm going to start by splitting you into groups – I want the singers to stand together in the far corner, the musicians by the stage steps, the comedians over here…"

When Miss Dubois had everyone organized into smaller groups, she decided to split the rehearsal, so that the singers and musicians would stay and the others would come back on Thursday lunchtime. As half the acts shuffled out, everything suddenly felt less panicky. Miss Dubois went through what each of the acts was planning to perform and then they each got a chance to rehearse. Once they'd finished she gave them some helpful feedback and a timed slot to turn up at the next rehearsal. Suddenly everything was running really smoothly.

"I think this idea of yours will work very well," Miss Dubois said, as the last act left the hall. "But what would have happened if I'd been held up today? Jas, you must take control, *oui*?"

Stage Fright

"I know, it's just all this organizational stuff … it's not really me." She tried to smile.

"Ah, but you have to make it so if you want this to be a success," Miss Dubois said firmly. "This is your show, not mine. I am just the helper here."

Jas nodded, biting her lip. "Um, Miss Dubois, I was thinking about my own act," she said, as we headed for the door. "I've been practising one of the solos from *Oliver!* for ages, so should I put my name down for a slot at the next rehearsal, too?"

Miss Dubois paused, frowning slightly. "I don't really think that would be right, Jas. You've just admitted how difficult it is for you to organize something like this – I think it needs all your focus. And how can you be on the judging panel and compete, too? It just wouldn't work. Now, come along or we'll be late for registration."

Jas stood there, speechless, as Miss Dubois headed off. There was no time to talk, so I gave Jas my most sympathetic smile and pulled her down the corridor. When we got to class, she slumped into her chair, looking disheartened.

"Good rehearsal?" Nisha asked.

Jas shook her head. "It's a disaster. Miss Dubois says

I can't be in the show myself. I had no idea that being involved in the talent show would mean I couldn't be in it. I mean, it wasn't exactly the *only* reason I set it up, but it was the main reason. Now it just seems like loads of hard work with none of the fun."

Me, Lexie and Nisha looked at each other as Jas drooped.

"I reckon you should just admit that directing isn't what you'd thought it would be and call it quits," Lexie suggested bravely.

"No way," Jas shot back. "I've been kicked off the play to make this work. If I back out now it'll have all been for nothing!"

As we made our way to English, I bumped into Georgie coming the other way.

"Are you coming to the rehearsal later?" she asked me.

"Yup," I nodded. "Can't wait!"

"Me neither," she said excitedly. "See you there!"

Jas rolled her eyes and looked even more grumpy. Jas's moods never usually lasted very long, but it seemed as though everything had changed since the *Oliver!* audition and I was beginning to get a bit tired of it. I remembered Dad's words about being my own person, so I took a deep breath, determined to tell her how I felt. "I'm not going to stop enjoying the play, Jas, just because you're not in it."

Jas's eyes nearly popped out of her head. She opened her mouth to speak, but no words came out, and as Lexie and Nisha caught up with us in the corridor she turned and stormed off. She barely said a word for the rest of the afternoon, and as soon as the bell went she announced that she was going home to work on the talent show and disappeared towards the cloakrooms. She was clearly stewing, but I decided not to make the first move this time – I'd done nothing wrong.

I headed to the lockers with Lexie and Nisha to put away our books.

"What time should we meet up in town on Saturday for our present-buying trip?" Nisha asked.

"About two?" I suggested.

"Perfect," Lexie agreed, closing her locker. "Maybe we could fit in a hot chocolate!"

"Defo!" me and Nisha said in unison, then burst out laughing. At that second, Jas came round the corner to the lockers. She saw us giggling and looked hurt for a second.

"Night," she said stiffly.

"Bye," we called back. I felt terrible and by the looks of it, so did Nisha and Lexie. I so wanted to make her feel better by telling her what we'd been giggling about, but that would have totally spoilt her surprise.

The rehearsal was amazing. Georgie and I spent most of the evening practising all the different techniques we'd learned and turning each other into the different characters in *Oliver!*.

"You're getting really good at this, Ellie," Claire said as she looked at my handiwork.

"Thanks," I said, blushing with pride.

When Dad picked me up I still looked like a street urchin, and, as I was explaining why, my phone suddenly barked, making me jump.

Gd rehearsal?

Gr8 thx. u ok? I replied.

R U, L & N fed up with me??? U huddling 2gether – am i missing something?

Stage Fright

I reread the message, wondering how to reply. I wanted to say that we were a bit fed up with her prima donna antics, but I couldn't say that by text. And as I couldn't explain the real reason for our huddling, I made up a little white lie:

Just talking, nothing else. All cool

The rest of the week raced by, and I was exhausted come Saturday, but I'd promised Mum I'd get up and make a start on my homework, as I would be spending all afternoon in town. After lunch, I pulled on my coat and slouchy boots, and grabbed my bag.

It felt strange getting ready to meet Lexie and Nisha without Jas, but I was excited to be going secret present shopping!

"Have you got any idea what you want to buy Jas?" Mum asked, as she backed the car out of the drive.

"Songs for her new karaoke machine," I said. "Hopefully it'll cheer her up."

"Is she still upset about the play?" Mum asked.

I nodded. "And now she can't even be in her

own talent show."

"Oh dear. Well, some karaoke songs sound like the perfect present," said Mum. "Then she can be a star anytime she wants!"

I grinned – Mum knew all about Jas's diva ways, so she understood the situation perfectly. We drove on into town until we came to the high street, where I'd arranged to meet Nisha and Lexie.

"There they are!" I said, as Mum pulled up.

"See you back here at four," she called as I jumped out. "Have a good time!"

As I ran over to Nisha and Lexie, my mobile started to ring. I fished about in my bag and then froze.

"It's Jas!" I said, panicking.

"Don't answer it!" Lexie said. "She'll get really suspicious!"

"Won't she be more suspicious if you don't answer it?" Nisha worried.

"Good point," I said, pressing the green button. "Hi, Jas!"

"Hey, Ellie," Jas said, "I wondered if you fancied coming round this evening? Mum says you can stay over if you like?"

"Sounds good," I said quickly. "I'll just need to

double check with Mum and give you a ring back."
Suddenly a car tooted.

"Where are you? Are you in town…?"

I made a face at the others "Uh, no … I mean, I am,"
I stuttered. "I mean, I came in with Mum."

"So you can ask her right now, then, can't you?"
Jas said sounding puzzled.

"She's just nipped off to … to the loo," I said,
making even more of a face as Lexie began to giggle,
which did NOT help! "I'll give you a ring back – in fact,
I'll ring back if she says no, if she says yes, I'll just see
you later!"

"OK, see you about six-ish?"

"Cool, see you then!" I ended the call and we all
burst out laughing.

"Phew, that was close!"

"Come on, let's get present hunting!" Nisha said,
linking arms with Lexie and me and dragging us down
the high street. First we headed for Anthems. Between
us we had enough money to buy Jas two compilation
DVDs for her karaoke machine. We looked through all
the different ones, then chose one full of classic
karaoke hits, and the other featuring bang-up-to-date
chart songs. Then we bought some sparkly wrapping

paper and a little bag to put them in and spent ages looking at cards. Lexie chose a jokey one, and I got one with a cute picture of a kitten that looked like Crumble. Nisha had already made hers, though she wouldn't tell us what was on the front. Then we headed to the diner for a hot chocolate. And although it was weird without Jas, it felt great to be able to talk about *Oliver!* without worrying.

Before I headed round to Jas's that night, I wrote my card and tucked it in her present bag at the bottom of my wardrobe. I smiled at the thought of how happy she'd be when she opened the DVDs, and how I'd probably have to listen to her perform every single song in one sitting. I was still smiling when I ran round the corner to her house that evening.

"What are you grinning about?" Jas finally asked as I tried and failed to perfect my poker face.

"Nothing!" I said, breaking into a giggle. She rolled her eyes, but my good mood seemed to be infectious, and in no time at all we were both giggling our heads off!

11

Kirsty sticks her oar in and Jas's forgetfulness has unexpected results...

On Monday morning I kept glancing at Lexie and Nisha, thinking about the secret that we shared and how happy Jas would be when she opened her present. I could tell that Nisha and Lexie were struggling to keep quiet, just like me. Jas kept giving us odd looks, which made us want to giggle more, but our smiles were soon cut short when Kirsty sashayed over in registration.

"Did you have a nice time in the diner on Saturday?" she asked, a wicked glint in her eye.

"What are you on about?" Jas tutted. "We weren't there on Saturday. You should get your eyes tested."

"Oh, sorry," Kirsty said, smirking as she saw me, Lexie and Nisha squirm. "I didn't mean you, Jas, I was talking to these three."

With that, Kirsty turned tail and went to sit down, glancing over her shoulder as Jas looked at us, utterly hurt. "I asked you if you were in town and you said no," she said as Miss Dubois started to take the register. "I knew you'd been acting all cliquey. Why didn't you just say if you didn't want me around?"

"Jas, it wasn't like that," Nisha whispered.

"Quiet, please," Miss Dubois said firmly. Beside me, I could feel Jas shaking. As soon as the register had been taken she stormed out, with me, Lexie and Nisha running after her. It was PE first thing, and we finally caught up with her in the changing rooms, getting ready in the corner. I heard a sniff as we hurried over.

"We better tell the truth," said Lexie.

Me and Nisha nodded, as we dashed past Kirsty, who was loving the drama she'd created.

"Jas, we only met up without you," I gabbled, as she wiped her nose on her sleeve, "because … well, because we were buying your birthday present. That's the only reason."

Jas looked up, biting her lip.

Stage Fright

"We wanted it to be a surprise," Nisha added as Jas's expression changed from one of misery to one of dismay.

"And I've ruined it," she sighed.

"You didn't," Lexie pointed out. "Kirsty did that."

"I'm sorry, though," Jas sniffed. "I just thought that, after the way everything's been recently, that you were fed up with me…"

At that moment Terrifying Townsend stalked in to get everyone moving, and roped Lexie and Nisha into fetching the sack of netballs. Lexie was about to protest, but one look at our PE teacher's face made her think better of it. Nisha gave Jas a concerned smile and ushered Lexie outside.

"I overheard Lexie calling me a diva the other day," Jas said quietly after they'd gone. I pulled on my kit and sat down next to her to do up my trainers. "Have I really been that bad?"

I was about to say "no", and be the peacemaker like I always had been, but I knew there was some truth in what Lexie had said, and I thought it might be good for Jas to hear it from her BFF.

"You *have* been a bit of a prima donna recently," I said, going a bit pink. "Not your usual fun self."

Jas bristled for a moment as everyone around us started to troop outside. "I've had lots of things going on, you know."

"You're not the only one who's busy, Jas," I said firmly. "Nisha's been spending loads of time helping Miss Malik with the scenery for *Oliver!*, and Lexie's had lots of sports stuff going on. But you've been so caught up with what *you're* doing that you haven't even noticed. The world doesn't always revolve around you, Jas."

Jas cringed. "Ouch! I sound horrible, even to me. Have I really been that bad?"

I nodded. "Kind of…"

Jas groaned. "It's since the play started, and then having the talent show on top – they've turned me into a monster! Thanks for being straight with me, though, as horrible as it is to hear."

"That's what BFFs are for," I smiled, pleased that I'd been brave enough to say something. "Come on, we better get going or Terrifying Townsend is going to kill us!"

"Ellie," Jas said, still looking a bit unsure, "you do all still want to come to my ice-skating party, don't you? It wouldn't be the same without you."

"You'll have to ask the other two," I said, acting

seriously for a second, "but there's no way you'd stop me!"

Jas linked arms with me as we headed outside. Nisha and Lexie saw us and headed over. "I'll ask them now," she said anxiously.

After Jas got a whack on the arm from Lexie as an "of course!" and a smile and a "yes" from Nisha, Jas was more relaxed, but if she thought her week was about to get better, she was seriously mistaken. At lunchtime the next day, we had another talent show rehearsal. Lexie and Nisha had already said they wouldn't be able to make it, and at breaktime, Georgie came to tell me that Claire had arranged a last-minute make-up and costume meeting with Mrs Crawfield.

"Sorry, Jas," I said, "but I can't miss this."

Jas looked panicky when she realized she'd be on her own, but she tried to hide it with a shrug and a smile. As the bell went for lunch, I scooted out of the door with Zophia and Molly, leaving Jas talking to Trin about her birthday party. I almost doubled back to remind Jas about the rehearsal, but thought better of it – I didn't want her to think I was fussing, and after

all, it wasn't as if she could actually forget her own rehearsal, was it?

After the meeting, I headed for the hall thinking that I might still be able to help Jas out. As I rounded the corner, I bumped straight into Nisha, coming the other way in a bit of a panic.

"What's up?"

"Have you seen Jas anywhere?"

I shook my head. "No, why?"

"She hasn't turned up for the rehearsal," Nisha explained. "Miss Dubois is hopping mad! I peeped in as I passed the hall on my back from the art studio and she asked me to go and look for her."

As we rushed back towards the foyer we saw Jas and Trin wandering down the stairs leading from the library, laughing.

"Jas!" I gasped. "Where have you been?!"

"Looking at a book on ice-skating ready for my party – Trin wanted to get some tips ahead of Saturday," she explained, frowning. "Why, where's the fire?!"

"Er, in the hall," I said, shaking my head, "with Miss Dubois!"

Stage Fright

Suddenly the penny dropped. Jas took off down the corridor, with me and Nisha in hot pursuit. She burst into the hall to find the rehearsal running smoothly.

"I'm so sorry, Miss Dubois," Jas began. "I forgot and—"

Miss Dubois did not look happy. She held up her hand, cutting Jas off.

"There are two more acts to run through," she said calmly. "We'll talk about this after the rehearsal's over."

We kept quiet until the final act left the stage. As the door swung shut, Jas turned to Miss Dubois, her eyes brimming with tears.

"I … I really am sorry, Miss Dubois," she quavered. "I just completely forgot…"

"Organizing something like this takes a lot of hard work and dedication," Miss Dubois said sternly, "as you are finding out. I said that I would help out with the show, Jas, because you told Mrs Crawfield how passionate you were about it. But you haven't done any planning, and today you failed to turn up, leaving everything to me. It's not good enough, Jas, it really isn't. I thought you had your heart set on this show?"

"I just wanted the chance to shine…" Jas said quietly.

Miss Dubois nodded. "Jas, I think it's clear that your

passion is for being *on* the stage, not directing others."

"But you and Mrs Crawfield make it look so easy," Jas sighed.

"Ah, well, that takes years of practice," Miss Dubois said, softening slightly. "It's a bit like being in the play, *non*? You think being in a lead role will be easy, but actually it's pretty scary at first, and it takes practice. Better to start in the chorus and build up to it."

At the mention of the play, Jas's shoulders slumped and a big tear spilled over and rolled down her cheek. "I can't believe I lost my place in the chorus. I'd do anything to be in the play again. I've messed everything up!"

"Not everything," Miss Dubois pointed out. "The talent show's really popular. But I think I should take it over now, *oui*?"

"Really?" Jas asked, looking relieved. Miss Dubois nodded.

"And perhaps if you apologize to Mrs Crawfield she might let you have your place back in the chorus?" Nisha suggested.

Jas looked up for a second, but then shook her head. "There's no way she'd let me back, not after the way I behaved," she sniffed.

Stage Fright

"Would you like me to have a word with her?" Miss Dubois asked. "I can see how much it means to you."

Jas's eyes widened as she looked at Miss Dubois hopefully. "Could you?" she asked. "Do ... do you really think she might listen?"

Miss Dubois smiled. "I can't promise anything, but I can ask. She looked at her watch. "I'm afraid it'll have to wait though, as the bell's about to go for afternoon lessons. Now, come on, all of you, or we'll be late for registration!"

Jas was in a state of nervous excitement for the rest of the afternoon.

"Do you think she'll say yes?" she whispered during art, our last lesson of the day.

"Hopefully," I said. Jas waited for a second.

"Do you think Miss Dubois has asked yet?" Jas whispered back again.

"I don't know!" I giggled. "Honestly, Jas, you've asked me about a hundred times already!"

Jas giggled too. We were supposed to be finishing off our Christmas cards, but most of us had pretty much given up on our efforts, apart from Nisha.

She was still putting the finishing touches to her stained glass window design, which looked stunning.

"That's so cool, Nisha," I said, full of admiration.

Jas leaned over. "Can I see? Oooh, that's gorgeous!"

Nisha grinned. "Thanks, guys! And I think I've just about finished," she said proudly, just as the bell went. We handed our efforts in to Miss Malik, and quickly packed up. We were just heading to the door with Nisha and Lexie when Miss Malik suddenly called out.

"Jas! I need a quick word."

Jas skulked back in, wondering what she could have got in to trouble for this time, but a moment later she returned grinning nervously. "Mrs Crawfield wants to see me. I've got to go to the staffroom – will you all come with me?"

"Of course!" Lexie laughed, linking her arm.

We rushed back to the foyer and up the stairs. As we neared the staff room, Jas crossed her fingers for luck and knocked on the door. Mr Wood appeared a moment later – he glared at Jas as she explained why she was there, then went to fetch Mrs Crawfield.

"Miss Dubois has spoken to me about how much you'd like to rejoin the cast," Mrs Crawfield said, giving Jas a stern look. Jas nodded.

Stage Fright

"I … I'm really, really sorry for being disruptive," she said earnestly. "But, I promise, I'd work so hard if you did let me have another chance."

"Well, good, because you'll have to," Mrs Crawfield said. Jas looked up, her eyes widening. "I expect you to be at rehearsals tonight – concentrating hard! I had asked Jarvis, the understudy for Oliver, to double up for Dodger, but if you promise to learn all the lines, you can have that role back, too. But I want no more distractions, Jas. I don't want to hear that you're headlining the talent show, OK?"

"You're serious?!" Jas squealed. "I can come back to the play?" Mrs Crawfield nodded. "I'll be the most dedicated cast member ever! I'll be amazing! No – I mean, I'll blend in – you won't even know I'm there!"

With that Jas turned and ran towards us, calling out a "thank you" to Mrs Crawfield over her shoulder and doing one of the moves from the "Food, Glorious Food" dance. As Mrs Crawfield turned to go back into the staffroom I saw that she was shaking her head and smiling.

12

Jas is restored to her normal cheery self and has a birthday bash – literally...

When we headed into school on Thursday, the Christmas vibe had appeared overnight – a massive Christmas tree, dripping with tinsel, baubles and flashing white fairy lights, greeted us in the foyer. It even had a pile of (fake) presents beneath the branches. Miss Dubois arrived in class carrying a huge box of decorations and we all helped transform the room into a glittering, shimmering grotto. By the end of the morning we were all feeling really Christmassy, and spent our lunchtime making Christmas present wishlists.

"I usually get joint Christmas and birthday

presents," Jas said, as she leaned over and saw the list Lexie had drawn up – including cross-country trainers, a hoody, new collars and leads for Smarty and Jinx, *and* loads of CDs. "That's the only trouble with having your birthday so close to Christmas."

"My list might look impressive," said Lexie, "but I won't get half of it!"

"It's a *wishlist*, remember!" Nisha laughed.

"In that case I'm putting down everything I can think of!" Jas giggled.

"Talking of birthdays, are you ready for your party on Saturday, Jas?" I asked.

"Pretty much. I've got my outfit sorted, and Mum's going to make a chocolate cake," she said excitedly. "The only thing I've got to do is tidy up for you three!" she added, pulling a face.

"Don't go to any trouble on my account," Lexie grinned.

Everything felt like it was back on track. Lexie and Jas were mates again, Jas was back in the play, we had a party to look forward to – and Christmas was just around the corner!

On Saturday morning, Lexie and Nisha came over to wrap Jas's present, then we raced round to her flat. It was really icy – the frost had covered the evergreen bushes with a glittery dust and turned the pavements all sparkly. It wasn't hard to miss where the birthday girl lived – there were pink, purple and white balloons tied to the gate, and a "Happy Birthday" banner over the door. We were just about to knock when the door was yanked open from the inside and Jas stood there, grinning like a Cheshire cat. She was dressed in thick stripy leggings and a short purple dress, with a huge badge pinned to the front, sporting the number "12".

"Happy birthday!" we chorused.

"Thanks!" she beamed. "Come and see what Mum, Josh and Lulu got me – it's totally fabulous!" We piled into the sitting room, where Jas already had her karaoke machine plugged in.

"No *Oliver!* songs on the playlist," she winked, "so I can't treat you to any of those! But it came with a few sample songs so I've got something to sing until I save up for some more." Nisha, Lexie and me exchanged a quick glance – we were all bursting to give Jas her present, but we'd made a pact to wait until after the skating party so we could make her day last as long as possible.

Stage Fright

Jas picked up the microphone, pressed play, and the karaoke machine burst into life, blaring out the first few bars of a Tulisa track.

Half an hour later, we were still singing along to the karaoke machine. Every so often Josh would appear and shake his head as if we were all totally sad, but even he couldn't dampen Jas's spirits today. I think she'd have been happy staying at home all day, if Gloria hadn't appeared to tell us we had to leave in five minutes to get to the ice rink. As we hurried out of the door, Josh held on to Lulu, who was wailing at being left behind.

"This is a giant favour I'm doing you!" he called, as he tried to pacify his baby sister.

"So sweet!" Jas giggled, pretending to take a picture.

Trin, Molly, Tabs, Maisie and Zophia were all waiting for us inside the entrance. We raced to change our shoes, then took what felt like an hour to lace up the boots, and even longer to wobble our way to the ice rink, our arms circling like windmills as we tried to balance on the thin blades.

"This is before we've even seen the ice!" Jas giggled as we finally made it to the rink.

"I'm so nervous!" Trin shivered, as she teetered by the edge, gripping it tightly.

"It's fun, just hold on to my arm," Lexie offered. "I've done it before."

The next second one foot slid from under her and Lexie crashed to the floor, giggling like mad as we all helped to haul her up. It didn't take long for us to get the hang of it, although there was still the occasional slide and scream. I was fine as long as I kept looking dead ahead. As soon as I glanced to the side to see how Jas was getting on, or tried to wave to Gloria, I lost my balance and toppled over on to the ice with a thud!

As Jas got more confident, she decided to perform the chorus moves and songs of *Oliver!*. She was doing well until she got a bit ambitious and tried to skate backwards. She ended up on the ice with her legs in the air and for a second she didn't move. We all skidded and wobbled over as fast as we could.

"Are you all right, Jas?" I gasped. She looked up and I saw tears streaming down her face. Then I realized that she was smiling. She managed a nod before bursting into a fresh fit of hysterical laughter, setting the rest of us off.

At that moment, the bell rang to signal the end of the session. I pulled Jas up, and we were both still laughing as we skated to the edge of the rink. We changed back into our shoes, which felt *so* comfortable after the skates, and headed up to the cafeteria.

After a delicious lunch of chicken and chips, Gloria got out Jas's birthday cake, which was decorated with twelve pink candles. We sang "Happy Birthday" at the top of our voices, and watched Jas blow out her candles and make a wish.

"Thanks so much for coming," she beamed at all of us.

"It's been the best fun ever," Zophia said.

I grinned. "We wouldn't have missed it for the world."

As soon as we got back to the flat, Josh handed Lulu back to Gloria and set off to his friend's house, anxious to avoid the "super-girly" evening, as he put it. We headed in to the lounge and Lexie fetched Jas's present.

"These are perfect!" she squealed, ripping off the

sparkly paper to reveal our karaoke DVDs. "Thanks so much, guys. Let's put one on now!"

"Hang on, there is one more thing," I said, and we all handed her our cards. Nisha looked on expectantly as Jas opened hers.

"Wow!" Jas squealed when she saw the picture Nisha had drawn on the front of the card. "I look like a real star!" she said, beaming. The picture was a portrait of Jas, wearing a sequinned dress and big sunglasses. Nisha smiled proudly as she saw Jas's reaction.

Jas drew the curtains and turned out most of the lights. For the rest of the afternoon we sang our way through almost all the tracks.

"Isn't this one of the songs Ajay and Dev are playing for the talent show?" Nisha asked, as she recognized the opening bars to "Love is Everything".

"Yes!" Jas said, spinning round with the mic. "I love this one!"

Every time the song ended Jas leaped up and pressed repeat until finally Lexie had had enough. "Stop!" she cried, "I can't take any more of this song. I'm going to be singing it in my sleep!"

We collapsed on the sofa to watch a DVD, and

Stage Fright

Gloria brought in slices of pizza and a big bowl of popcorn. It was a brilliant end to a perfect day.

"Thanks again for helping to make this the best birthday ever," Jas said sleepily as the film came to an end. We got out our sleeping bags and laid them all out on the floor.

"It's been so much fun," I agreed, giggling as I remembered Jas spinning on the ice.

"Fun?!" Lexie squeaked. "I'm going to be covered in bruises tomorrow!"

"I think I am already!" Nisha added.

"And, I just wanted to say," Jas said, slightly hesitantly, "I'm really sorry for being such a pain this half term."

"At least you're bearable again now," I smiled. "Just."

The next second I felt a pillow whack my head. I squealed and grabbed a cushion and thwacked Jas back. Then Lexie and Nisha joined in the pillow fight, and we only stopped when Gloria finally put her head round the door and reminded us that Lulu was asleep. After that we carried on talking in hushed whispers until finally settling down to sleep.

When we got back to school on Monday, we all compared our ice-skating bruises until Miss Dubois arrived.

After she finished taking the register, she called for everyone's attention. "I have a couple of announcements to make," she said, smiling round the class. "Firstly, the Christmas card competition. I'm very happy to announce that the Year Seven winner is someone from Kingfisher. Nisha – your card will be going into print. Very well done!" Miss Dubois held up the winning design for everyone to see.

"Brilliant, Nisha!" Lexie cried.

"I've never won anything before!" Nisha beamed.

"It'll be on sale in the foyer in a few days' time," Miss Dubois continued, "along with the winning cards from the other years. And secondly, before you all rush off to PE, I've got one more piece of news. As you all know, Jas had an idea for a talent show."

Jas bit her lip, looking uncertain about whether to be proud or embarrassed.

"Well, lots of you suggested the talent show as the theme for the junior disco," said Miss Dubois, pointing at the suggestions box on her desk. Me and Jas exchanged glances – with so much else going on, we'd forgotten all about the junior disco. "And that is the winning theme!" she went on. "The talent show performance will be part of the disco, so we're in for a wonderful night of entertainment!"

As we left the room, everyone was talking about how exciting the junior disco would now be. By the time we reached the changing rooms for PE, some people were even speculating that it might beat the senior disco in the cool stakes!

The rest of the week flew by, and the *Oliver!* rehearsals cranked up about ten gears. The lead roles met most lunchtimes, and we had rehearsals four nights out of five, ahead of the dress rehearsal the following Monday night. Dad even let me skip my Friday swimming practice for the costume run-through.

As I stood watching from the side of the stage, I was amazed by how professional everyone was – especially Amelia and Daniel. When the run-through finished, the whole cast buzzed with excitement as it sank in how close we were to the performances. Mrs Crawfield announced that the dress rehearsal on Monday afternoon would be performed to the rest of the

school, followed by the real performances on Tuesday and Wednesday evening. To make things even more nerve-racking, Mr Flight announced that both nights were a sell-out!

On Saturday morning, Jas and I hooked up with Lexie and Nisha in town to do some Christmas shopping. The high street was decorated with strings of lights criss-crossing the road and at one end was a huge, tinsel-laden Christmas tree. A brass band stood to one side, stomping their feet to keep warm as they played "The Holly and the Ivy". We decided to split up to buy presents for each other, but we all headed for the same shops and kept bumping into each other! After I'd bumped into Nisha for the second time we gave up, and I texted Jas and Lexie, telling them to meet us at the diner.

As we sat sipping our hot chocolates, complete with tiny marshmallows, and making plans for Christmas, I couldn't help smiling to myself. It was hard to believe what a difference a half term made – just a few weeks ago I'd never felt so miserable, but now I was happier than ever!

"Does anyone know who the understudy is?" And the play goes LIVE!

The whole school was buzzing on Monday morning – partly because it was the last week before we broke up for Christmas, and partly because it was the day of the dress rehearsal! Lexie was at an inter-school cross-country competition that morning, but Terrifying Townsend had promised to have them back "in good time". At lunchtime, Jas, Nisha and me headed for the dining hall, but we were so excited we could barely manage to eat a thing. The cast has been told to gather in the hall straight after lunch and by the time we arrived, lots of the cast were already there, laughing and joking, a mixture of nerves and excitement.

"Can you see Lexie anywhere?" Nisha asked, scanning the room.

I shook my head. "Not yet, but I'm sure the bus will be back soon – Terrifying Townsend would never be late."

Mr Flight arrived and started to get everyone organized. Nisha and Jas went off to change into their costumes and I joined Claire at the make-up tables, which had been set up in the far corner of the hall. She was doing Amelia's make-up, applying false eyelashes and lipstick and some rouge on her cheeks. Amelia kept turning round in her chair and glancing at the hall doors.

"Where's Daniel?" she finally asked. "Shouldn't he be here by now?"

"He's been doing the cross-country competition this morning," I said, "with my friend Lexie, who's in the chorus. There's no sign of them yet."

Amelia frowned and looked at her watch. "We're due to start in fifteen minutes. If they don't hurry up, we might have to use the understudy." An anxious look crossed her face. "It's a Year Seven, isn't it?"

"It's Jas – Jasmine Cole," I said, going bright pink as Amelia turned her long-lashed eyes on me.

"Is she good?"

Stage Fright

I nodded. I desperately wanted to rush over to Jas, but at that second Mrs Crawfield appeared at the front of the stage and clapped her hands. A hush descended. Everyone stopped what they were doing and looked up.

"We've got about five minutes before we're due to go on," she announced, "but we're missing our Artful Dodger and one of the chorus – the coach bringing them back from the cross-country competition has broken down. That means the Artful Dodger understudy will have to step in. Jas?"

Jas stepped forward, unable to stop a grin from spreading across her face.

"Are you ready for this?" Mrs Crawfield asked.

Jas nodded. "Definitely!"

"Great! The curtain goes up in ten minutes. Just do your best."

Jas was about to turn away, when Mrs Crawfield called her back. "And remember to enjoy yourself!"

"I will," Jas grinned.

"Right, can we have all the cast backstage, please!" Mrs Crawfield called out.

"Is this really happening?" Jas breathed, as me and Nisha rushed up to congratulate her. "Pinch me now!"

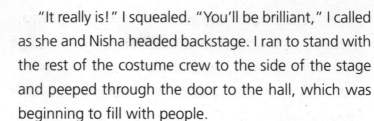

"It really is!" I squealed. "You'll be brilliant," I called as she and Nisha headed backstage. I ran to stand with the rest of the costume crew to the side of the stage and peeped through the door to the hall, which was beginning to fill with people.

A few minutes later, the lights dimmed and the chattering in the hall stopped as the first notes of "Food, Glorious Food" sounded out. The next second the thick, heavy curtains swung open and the performance began.

The audience giggled as some of the actors found themselves on the wrong side of the stage and had to quickly scoot round the back of the chorus. A couple of people forgot their lines but Mr Flight, who had the job of prompt, soon got things going again. Then Oliver arrived in London, and suddenly it was Jas's turn to step into the spotlight. She stood in the wings on the other side of the stage waiting for her cue, then stepped on to the stage, her scruffy top hat tilted jauntily.

Jas began to speak in a broad Cockney accent. She was word-perfect, even if she wasn't in quite the right place and Lewis had to subtly nod his head to direct her a couple of times. Then she burst into "Consider Yourself" and she was off, making the audience giggle as she pulled faces and danced round Oliver. Nisha appeared by my side and danced back on to the stage with the rest of the chorus. When the song finished the audience cheered wildly. Jas came off beaming like never before, but she didn't have long to relax before she was straight into "You've Got to Pick a Pocket or Two".

"You're amazing!" I cried, giving Jas a hug after the curtain was drawn for the interval.

"Thanks, Ellie!" she beamed, wiping her forehead. "I'm shaking – it's so much more nerve-racking than I thought!"

All the leads patted her on the back as they trooped past and Mrs Crawfield gave her a thumbs up. Then Daniel and Lexie appeared, leaping up the steps into the wings. They'd watched the last five minutes of the first half from the back of the hall. "Not bad for a Year Seven," Daniel grinned, tipping Jas's hat.

"I can't believe I missed you!" Lexie said.

"Right," Mrs Crawfield called out. "Now you're here, Daniel, you better take over for Act Two. Very well done, Jas," she said. "How was it?"

"Honestly?" Jas asked. "*Terrifying*! I mean, it was brilliant today, in front of the school, but when it's in front of parents…?" Jas gave a shiver.

"So you don't mind me taking over?" Daniel asked, grinning.

Jas shook her head. "No way!"

"But what if I get sick tomorrow?" Daniel piped up. "You'll have to do it then."

"You will NOT get sick," Jas giggled, "and that's an order! I'm going back to the chorus, and that's where I'll stay!"

A few minutes later, Mr Flight sounded the backstage bell. "Positions, please – the second half is about to start!"

The rest of the play flew by and suddenly the final song drew to a rousing finish and the cast walked on to take their bows. I watched Jas looking out over the audience and lapping up the applause. She glanced sideways at me and grinned. As everyone filed off the stage you could feel the excitement. Jas was the centre of a crowd of performers, all congratulating her.

Then Josh appeared behind the curtain, a huge grin on his face.

"My little sis," he said. "That was awesome. Hear that? Because I'm so not going to repeat it."

Stage Fright

Miss Dubois had trouble settling everyone down in registration on Tuesday morning. With so much excitement about *Oliver!* no one could concentrate on sitting still or listening for more than about ten seconds.

"Silence, everyone, please!" she said in a raised voice. "Please remember that school hasn't broken up for the holidays just yet!"

As the day wore on, the buzz escalated to fever pitch. And when last bell finally sounded, the four of us charged out of the room, heading for the hall.

Abbie and her team helped everyone with their costumes, before sending them to Claire's make-up station. I was working on the chorus so I got to do the make-up for Jas, Lexie and Nisha. The performers' nerves were starting to kick in now – some people were walking backwards and forwards, joking about, while others were deadly silent.

"Attention, everyone," Mrs Crawfield called, "the doors are open and the hall is filling up, so we need to keep the noise level down!"

I looked over to where Jas, Lexie and Nisha were waiting by the edge of the stage, peeping round the curtain. Jas caught me looking over and made a

pretend scared face and wobbled her knees. Somewhere out there Mum and Dad would be sitting with Gloria!

Mr Flight dashed by. "Five minutes! Five minutes, everyone. Can I have you all in position, please?"

"Good luck!" Max called out to everyone in a loud whisper. "Let's make this performance the best ever!"

The audience gave the cast a rousing round of applause as they lined up on stage for their curtain call. When Amelia and Max came on the clapping got even louder, but Daniel got the biggest cheer of the night. As the curtain came down again Jas ran off the stage, grinning from ear to ear.

"That was the best fun *ever*!" she said. "I want to do it again!"

"And so you will," Mr Flight laughed. "Same time tomorrow night! Good performance, everyone!"

As soon as Jas was changed we said goodbye to Nisha and Lexie and rushed into the hall to find our parents.

"Well done, Jas! That was brilliant!" said Dad, "and I hear you make a pretty mean Dodger, too!"

Stage Fright

"Thanks! I've had so much fun," Jas said. She beamed as Gloria gave her a huge hug.

"And the make-up was fantastic, Ellie," said Mum. "You both did a great job."

"Come on then, superstars," said Dad. "You must be exhausted. Especially you, Jas, after all that leaping about!"

"I am!" Jas grinned. "But I'm way too excited to sleep!"

The talent show rocks, in a totally unexpected way!

The play went amazingly again the next night, and I wanted the evening to go on for ever. But once it was over, everyone started to get excited about the disco – and the talent show. When the final bell buzzed on Thursday, we all flew home to give us as much time as possible to get ready before heading back. Lexie, Nisha and Jas came back to my house to get changed.

We went into my bedroom and I put on Jas's favourite song, "Love Is Everything". We knew the lyrics off by heart after Jas's birthday karaoke, so we all sang along.

"I'm so glad I was involved in the play," I smiled as

Stage Fright

I pulled on my thick purple sparkly tights. "Even if it *was* behind the scenes. Now I've seen what it's like I might even try for the chorus next year!"

"You should do!" Nisha beamed, pulling on a purple spotty dress. "It's amazing!"

"And I'm just so happy I didn't miss out completely," Jas smiled sheepishly, "by thinking that the chorus wasn't enough. It was brilliant!"

I helped everyone put on a tiny bit of eyeliner and lip gloss, just like I'd learned from Claire. We brushed our hair, checked ourselves out in my mirror, then jumped in Dad's car for a lift back to school.

"Welcome girls," Terrifying Townsend said jovially as we stepped in through the school entrance.

"Er, hello," Lexie mumbled back as we rushed past her into the main hall, where the music was already thumping.

"It's really dark!" Nisha gasped, pushing the doors open.

"Wow!" I whispered. Inside there were big glitter balls hanging from the ceiling, the tinsel decorating all the huge windows and disco lights swirling round the

vast space. The stage curtains were drawn back and there were bright fairy lights trailing all round it and above the stage hung a big, painted banner with "Talent Show" painted on in bright colours.

The hall was already filling up with groups of Year Sevens and Eights. We'd had discos at Woodview, but they'd been during the day and were much smaller. Even with just the juniors it was pretty huge. I noticed Kirsty and Eliza looking glamorous with their matching hairstyles and fake eyelashes. They were standing in the corner, giggling with their heads together, sipping drinks and looking everyone up and down. When a small group of Year Eight boys wandered past, looking a bit awkward, Kirsty and Eliza burst into a fresh fit of loud giggles and whispered to each other.

"Come on, let's get a drink," Lexie said, moving over to the table set out in the back corner, filled with bottles of Coke and lemonade and bowls brimming with crisps. As Miss Malik poured out our drinks, Zophia, Molly, Tabitha and Trin rushed up to us.

"This is so cool!" Molly beamed.

"Have you seen Wiggy?" Trin giggled. "Over by the corner?"

We looked through the dim lighting and saw Wiggy

in the corner with a mobile disco set. He was wearing a huge pair of earphones and his hair looked wonkier than ever!

"How did we miss him?" I laughed. We all stood together, watching from the edge of the hall as some of the Year Eight girls began to dance, while the boys messed about and raced around.

After we'd finished our plates of food, Jas and Lexie began to dance. Jas grabbed my arm and twirled me round. I felt myself go pink, feeling self-conscious, but then Nisha and the others joined in awkwardly and after a few minutes I stopped thinking about whether everyone was looking at us and started to relax.

The next second we heard a tapping echo round the hall. We looked round and saw Miss Dubois standing in the centre of the stage, holding a microphone.

"Good evening, everyone!" she called out. "It's time for you all to welcome the first act of our very own talent show! Put your hands together for Marcia and her hula hoops!"

Everyone cheered and whistled, gathering nearer the stage. As Marcia came out she took a bow, then began to hula like mad as everyone clapped in time to the music. Even when she dropped a few everyone just

kept cheering. Next up was Ed, who had everyone in stitches with his impressions. He was a natural behind the microphone and even Wiggy managed a smile when he realized that Ed was mimicking him. Miles told his jokes – he remembered the punchlines this time, but they were pretty terrible and he had everyone groaning. He was followed by Sam, performing his magic tricks. He'd obviously been practising really hard and even had a glamorous assistant (who turned out to be his sister) to hold his props for him.

"It's really nice that everyone's had a chance," I heard a Year Eight girl behind me say.

"Exactly," the girl next to her agreed, "and no one seems embarrassed at getting up there because it's just Years Seven and Eight. It's a really cool theme!"

I turned and saw that Jas was glowing.

"It's a hit!" I grinned, nudging her.

She nodded. "I *so* wish I was up there, though," she said, watching Saskia, Nemone and a few of their friends from Peregrine performing a daring cheerleading display.

We all stood and applauded the acts until it got to the last one. Ajay, Dev and Travis took to the stage with their guitars. They started to play and everyone cheered as they recognized the first couple of bars of Jas's favourite song, "Love Is Everything". Suddenly, as I watched the crowd all tapping their feet to the song's intro, I had an idea.

"Jas!" I shouted above all the noise. She looked round at me, her eyes sparkling. "You could be their lead singer! You know all the words – quick, go up there!"

Jas's eyes widened. "Seriously?"

"Of course!" Lexie jumped in. "It makes total sense!"

"They need a singer and you know all the words!" Nisha agreed.

"Go, get up there, quick!" I said, laughing.

Jas suddenly laughed. "OK, OK! But if I'm going up there, so are you three!"

"No way!" I said quickly.

"Ellie, that wasn't a question!" Jas said, looking determined. Nisha and Lexie were beaming. "Come on, it'll be fun! You said you fancied getting up on stage…"

Jas was right. I began to giggle as I let her take my arm. "I can't believe I'm doing this," I whispered as we quickly dived through the crowds and leaped up on to the stage.

Ajay grinned, nodding his approval. Jas took the mic but I stood, frozen for a second, looking down at the sea of faces. Then, as she began to belt out the first line, Lexie waved for me to come nearer and I stepped up to the mic with them. Jas sang, swirling her hair and dancing on the spot and I softly joined in with Lexie and Nisha. The audience were waving their hands in the air and singing along.

By the time we reached the chorus I had stopped feeling shy and started to sing louder, even putting in a few moves alongside the other three. I couldn't believe it – I was standing on stage alongside my three BFFs, looking out over a crowd of Year Sevens and Eights, not to mention teachers – and I was singing! That was something I never, ever thought would happen. Maybe joining drama club had changed me, just like Jas predicted. I'd grown more confident, even if I hadn't grown in height! I looked across to Jas. She looked happier than I had ever seen her – she was having her moment in the spotlight after all, and I was there to share it with her.

As Ajay, Dev and Travis played the final chords, the four of us looked across at each other, smiling like mad.

We headed for the steps to leave the stage. "I told

you this half term was going to be amazing!" Jas grinned. She was right – we might still be Year Sevens, but finally it felt like we were part of the school.

"I never dreamed that I'd say this," I smiled, "but Priory Road totally rocks!"

"Did someone mention rocks?" Wiggy asked, his headphones round his neck. It took us a second before we realized that he was actually joking, then we burst into laughter and began to dance. This term had been a real success and right now I couldn't wait for the next one to start!

Have you read?

Holly Robbins

BFFs

Sink or Swim

Me and my BFF, Jas, are moving up to secondary
school and I've got a zillion **MAJOR FEARS**…
Like looking a total dork in my **MASSIVE**
uniform … being teased about my
EMBARRASSING surname … and getting
completely **LOST** on my way to lessons!
And I'm sure I'll be one of the youngest
(and shortest) in the **WHOLE** school.

But my biggest, most **HUMONGOUS** fear
of all is that Jas will realize that I'm not cool
and find herself a new BFF.

*I think I need a popularity makeover
- and fast!*